By Michael Cadnum

PERIL ON THE SEA

MICHAEL CADNUM

PERIL ON THE SEA

FARRAR, STRAUS AND GIROUX
NEW YORK

Copyright © 2009 by Michael Cadnum
All rights reserved
Distributed in Canada by Douglas & McIntyre Ltd.
Printed in the United States of America
Designed by Jay Colvin
First edition, 2009
1 3 5 7 9 10 8 6 4 2

www.fsgteen.com

Library of Congress Cataloging-in-Publication Data
Cadnum, Michael.
Peril on the sea / by Michael Cadnum.— 1st ed.
   p.   cm.
Summary: In the tense summer of 1588, eighteen-year-old Sherwin Morris,
after nearly perishing in a shipwreck, finds himself aboard the privateer Vixen,
captained by the notorious and enigmatic Brandon Fletcher who offers him
adventure and riches if Sherwin would write and disseminate a flattering account
of the captain's exploits.
   ISBN-13: 978-0-374-35823-5
   [1. Pirates—Fiction.   2. Armada, 1588—Fiction.   3. Adventure and adventurers—
Fiction.   4. Great Britain—History—Elizabeth, 1558–1603—Fiction.]   I. Title.

PZ7.C11724Pe 2009
[Fic]—dc22

2008005421

For Sherina

More than anything
bright points of

yet to bloom
daffodils

PREFACE

THIS BOOK is a work of fiction but is in many essential ways true.

Many of the characters are based on people who actually lived. The Lord Admiral Howard was a real person, and so was Sir Francis Drake, and the celebrated privateers John Hawkins and Martin Frobisher. Many of the places are real, too, from the seacoast village of Beer to the famous ports of Plymouth and Southampton, and while I take liberties with the placement of manor houses and goose pens, the windswept cliffs of the south coast and the men and women who lived there are based on reality.

What is even more important, the attack of the Armada actually took place, and the adventures of the improvised navy Queen Elizabeth pulled together to defend her realm are as I depict them.

While my main characters are creations of my own imagination, the world they live in is built from the stuff of actual tumult.

In talking with veterans of wars of our own era, I have been struck by how vivid the memories are. Naval battles have stormed, comrades have lost their lives, and gunfire has obliterated the future. These events have taken place accompanied by heightened sensations of both horror and wonder that leave the surviving witnesses forever altered.

When we take part in history, we are at the same time experiencing our personal, subjective lives, and sometimes fighting simply to survive. It is this sense of personal ordeal and individual triumph that drove me as I wrote this story, just as it fuels my friendship for my characters, my respect for their courage, and my admiration for their loyalty to life.

I

INFERNO

I

SHERWIN MORRIS woke to the smell of fire.

Heavy seas had been building all day, and now the merchant ship *Patience* was standing to, the ship set sideways against the wind and the sea swells that rocked her.

Sherwin could hear Captain Pierson on deck, the ordinarily good-humored ship's master calling out, asking why the fire was still burning after the entire watch had been sent below to smother it.

Sherwin squeezed out of his narrow bunk, pulled on his doublet, thrust his cap onto his head, and joined the captain on deck. The night was thick with smoke, despite the strong wind that raked the ocean around them.

Recent hours had been troubling enough. The *Patience* had been dogged by an unfamiliar ship just visible on the horizon during the previous blustery day's sail, an English ship, by all reckoning, but one unknown to the captain, and all day Sherwin had sensed increasing anxiety in the cargo ship's crew.

But no one had anticipated this.

As soon as Sherwin saw the flames licking through the grate over the cargo hold he felt sick. The *Patience* was three days out of Hamburg, the thriving German-speaking port. The ship was laden with wine, a notoriously flammable cargo, but one that rarely caught fire, due to the skill of English coopers and the fact that there was usually enough briny leakage in the hold to discourage it.

Captain Pierson caught the look of concern in Sherwin's eye, and he gave a nod. "Lend a hand there, Sherwin, if you will," he said. The captain had agreed to train Sherwin—a youthful gentleman—in the fine points of shipboard life, and in exchange Sherwin was going to pen a history of Captain Pierson's voyages, with a publisher on Paternoster Row near Saint Paul's already secured.

But his duties also included helping the crew, especially in an emergency. Sherwin joined the gathering of hands on deck, manning a pump to draw water out of the English Channel and down into the fiery hold. As the pump water spewed and guttered into the increasing blaze, Sherwin could sense the fear of death seize his shipmates, among them Risley, the ship's cooper, with his hearty laugh silenced for the moment, and Wyman, the ship's gunner, laboring beside Sherwin with a prayer to Lord Jesus.

The moment might have been the span of a few heartbeats, or it might have been a quarter of an hour.

Sherwin had no way of reckoning the passage of time.

And in a way he had no desire to. This was, after all, the sort of experience eighteen-year-old Sherwin had sought in signing on with the well-regarded merchant captain—that, and the chance to earn money and a portion of public notice with the adventure he was intending to publish.

There was, furthermore, a sense of companionship rooted in the effort to save the ship that captivated Sherwin. Ship's boy and grizzled veteran alike, they all labored in a highly disciplined passion—more pumps brought into play, axes tearing at the decking, First Officer Timm calling out for the boatswain.

And then an explosion ripped the dark.

2

THERE WERE TWO BLASTS, actually, although in Sherwin's mind they seemed like one single event.

The first was a heat-rich heave of air, a gust ripe with the smell of burning oak and seething brandywine. Risley let out a groan, and Wyman shouted into Sherwin's ear, "Cling to the ratlines, lad."

Then the second explosion shattered timbers and flung snaking lengths of cordage, and this second blast stunned Sherwin with its intensity and gave him an instant, sick realization that no vessel could survive such violence.

The *Patience* lurched upward, and sideways, the deck splitting, flaming liquid spewing in spirals through the dark. Sherwin did as he had been advised and clung to the webbed ropes. The ratlines were themselves smoking, surprisingly, and he continued to cling even when the ropes caught fire around him, the tar and hempen fibers giving way to flame.

Sherwin felt the vessel lurch to starboard. Men were

leaping into the water by then, and the sea was steaming as flaming splinters of spruce rained down. Few sailors could swim—the knowledge was not widely learned. But Sherwin had been raised among rivermen and swan poachers, a gentleman's son taught by neighbors to swim like a water spaniel.

He released his grip on the burning ratlines and half fell, half leaped into the darkness.

The distance was greater than he had anticipated. The ship cast a reflection on the water, and he could make out the vivid image as flames reached up into the stays and gathered canvas of the sails above.

When he struck the water at last, he plunged deep, far below the surface. Not only was the early summer sea colder than Sherwin had expected, the water was saltier, stinging his eyes. His wool breeches and doublet were instantly leaden with brine, and Sherwin kicked back toward the surface, feeling the weight of his belt and his heavy linen shirt dragging him down.

He worked frantically to escape his clothing. Twenty sailors thrashed about on the surface, and then half that many, howling and swallowing water, some of the men going down with desperate dignity, others bawling and sputtering until the last moment.

On the crippled ship above, a boat hung on its davits, lowering down into the sea. A lurch of the ship caused the boat to empty her passengers, and Sherwin called out in horror as Captain Pierson plunged into the water.

The captain sank, and he did not reappear.

Sherwin had heard tales of ships going under, and had heard his ale-drinking companions recount the many times a sinking craft had sucked down sailors, drawing them in as surely as a swirling drain. Sherwin put his swimming powers to use, fighting to win distance between himself and the burning ship.

Small, darting creatures scouted outward from the vessel, rats in flight. Sherwin was relieved to hear the sounds of other men in the water, struggling to stay alive.

The *Patience* burned until, outlined in flame, she slipped heavily downward into the deep.

3

WITH A BOILING HISS of steam, the burning ship sank into the wind-whipped water and vanished.

The churning sea that followed her passage downward was pocked with spars and barrels, entire casks erupting into the starlight, to float intact on the black surface.

Nearly naked, and increasingly cold, Sherwin was shivering, the chill taking all sensation from his hands and feet. He swam toward one of the scattered, bobbing barrels and heaved his body over the rounded dome of a cask.

If nothing else, this largely fragmented cargo was proof that until moments before a protective ship had offered shelter. A wet and sinuous shape darted up out of the water, clinging to Sherwin's shoulder, and he gave a shout as he seized a frenzied rat and hurled the creature back into the dark.

He clung to the barrel for a long time, and felt that the passage of hours had ceased. Sherwin was tempted to envy his companions who were already in the merciful presence of their Lord.

He prayed with cold-stiffened lips, begging Jesus to keep the souls of his shipmates in peace, and grant him a further lease on life. His teeth snapped with the chill. His limbs were cramped, and even as he gripped the barrel the floating object dodged and lurched, rolling with a sullen heaviness, and he nearly fell back into the sea.

The swells continued, long, wind-lashed summits that from the ship had been little more than welcome proof that the weather was driving the *Patience* toward Southampton. By morning the ship would have been close enough to receive a pilot, sent out from shore to guide the vessel homeward, and Sherwin's first sea voyage, however brief, would have been accomplished.

Sherwin recalled his father's last words before the fever took his life—the barely audible "Sherwin, fear no man."

This farewell, not two months past, now seemed both wonderful and too brief. Sherwin saw that men were not to be feared nearly as much as the sea, against which no human power could stand.

He was aware of the cruelty of his situation—so near to surviving, but so hopeless at the same time. He had seen rivermen fished from the Thames succumb to cold even after their blue and shivering bodies had been plied with warm cider and the exhortations of loving friends. He believed that long before dawn his limbs would have lost all sensation, and his mind would have grown as numb and blank as every other part of his shriveled form.

This was most likely his last instant of mental clarity,

and he was already given reason to doubt his own sanity: because surely the vision that parted the swells was a hallucination, formed by an alloy of horror and desperate faith. Surely there could be no real ship, showing only storm sails against the driving wind, bearing down on the scattered remnants of the *Patience*?

Despite a doubt so strong it was like certain knowledge, Sherwin undertook an experiment.

He cried out.

He took a deep, shuddering breath and called out again, aware that no one could hear such a thin, ragged sound.

4

HIS VOICE was a small, bleak noise, not enough to call attention from this unknown ship.

The vessel followed the swells, her reduced sails cutting an angled shape out of the stars, a fighting ship, thought Sherwin, judging by her tall sterncastle and robust build. As the ship swept forward with the increasing wind, Sherwin could make out the row of gunports along her side, each port shuttered tightly against the sea.

Sherwin discerned the silhouettes of sailors, and the solitary figure on the quarterdeck of this vessel. Sherwin called again, a wordless cry, only to hear how duminutive his voice continued to sound under the great sky. He called, and he saw how far away the ship was, even now.

Even as Sherwin thanked God for his deliverance, he had the painful thought that this heedless vessel might simply part the litter on the sea and pass on toward Southampton. It could be on some errand of state, conveying a message, perhaps, regarding the Spaniards, rumored to be preparing a war against England.

The month was July of the year 1588. The previous year,
Sir Francis Drake had led a raid on the Spanish harbor
of Cádiz, and ever since, rumors of war had boiled along
the English coastline. Some supposed that a great invad-
ing force, carried by an Armada of warships, was sure to
set sail for English waters from Spain. Drake and other
privateers—mariners granted license by Queen Elizabeth and her Admiralty to attack and rob the Queen's
enemies—had continued to harass Spanish shipping,
and every port simmered with the desire to make profitable use of what peace remained.

Never before had Sherwin felt the smallness of his own
cry, the puniness of his own mortal life as he now called
out, "In the name of Jesus, look here, good sailors, here!"

The unfamiliar ship did slow her onward rush, it was
true, and she turned to, and at the sight of this maneuver
Sherwin was certain that his voice had been heard. A
boathook flashed, and with a prick of bitterness Sherwin
realized the nature of this ship's occupation. The vessel
was probing for intact casks—scavenging.

He also had a flicker of suspicion regarding this ship.
Privateers were little more than legal pirates, and as a
lawyer's son Sherwin had a high regard for the courage of
Drake and Hawkins, Fletcher and Frobisher—all of them
adventurers worthy of public acclaim—but he had no
such regard for their ethics.

Furthermore, there was no proof that this ship even
sailed with a privateer's regard for morals. In an English
navy that was largely informal, with so many freelance

fighting ships and freebooting adventurers, there were tales of hostages taken and innocent lives lost in the quest for gold. Torture on the high seas was rumored, and tales of innocent throats cut.

But Sherwin's choices were poor. The chill had seized every part of his body, and his eyes were slow in responding to his will, his lids sluggish and heavy, the eyeballs themselves turning slowly in their sockets. He had, at best, scant minutes to live.

He took his future into his hands. He kicked free of the cask and swam toward the ship. Even when he was close and the vessel loomed high over him, his voice was feeble compared with the groan and creak of timbers and lines.

Sherwin could smell the ship, an atmosphere of tar and gunpowder clinging about her hull. The sound of voices reached Sherwin, and the boathook flashed in the starlight, searching among the shattered casks.

A voice called, "By God, there's a rat the size of a Christian."

A lantern was held out and over the water, and this same voice broke into a laugh. A boathook was guided downward and Sherwin seized it, his fingers numb and unable to grip the long span of wood. He flung an arm over it and hung on, only to slip off and spin downward, releasing a long tendril of bubbles—his last, unanswered prayer.

I I
TEMPEST

5

KATHARINE WESTING braved the windy weather, hurrying at her father's side. Despite his limp, her father was an energetic man and always set Katharine a brisk pace. Their servingman Baines followed behind, at a respectful distance.

The night was blustery and a gale was building from across the Channel. Sir Anthony Westing leaned against his walking stick and let his gaze sweep the view from the clifftop, the chalk-and-shingle shore, the lace of breaking waves, and the salt sea beyond.

They came here often to fix their eyes on the horizon and to hope. While the shoreline of the Fairleigh estate offered no formal harbor, it was a safe anchorage situated between the village of Beer to the east and Sidmouth to the west on the Devonshire coast of southwestern England.

Often in recent months they had spied a ship in the distance that looked like the *Rosebriar*—several ships resembled her, including several Dutch vessels. But regardless of their high hopes, the sails they saw were never those of their long-awaited treasure.

This sea held their future, whether good or ill, as often before. Katharine loved the ocean as much as her father did, and loved to hear her father tell the stories of his days building pinnaces for the Admiralty, of the investments he had made as a speculator in spices and rare cloths, and of ships that had weathered brutal gales to arrive packed with answered prayers. Pinnaces were smaller vessels carried or towed by ships and used in exploration and surprise attacks, and a well-built pinnace was a craft of beauty.

This windy night she had been eager to sit before a fire and serve her father hot wine, and she had questioned the wisdom of going to church for the evening's service. But the ceremony was a tradition along the Devonshire coast, calling for the blessing of God on the vessels of fishermen and merchants alike, and this evening had included a sermon on the storm of the Sea of Galilee, and how Jesus had quieted the tempest with a command.

Katharine knew that her father was no more pious than the next man, but she also knew that no one was more in need of Heaven's favor than the two of them. His injured leg was not healing, and every day his limp had been growing more pronounced. Katharine was increasingly responsible for running the household. When problems arose, the servants told Katharine before they troubled her father with the news.

They had nearly reached the gatehouse of Fairleigh, the manor house and walled gardens of the dwindling Westing property, when the sound of hooves swept down on them from the woodland. The lead horse had a distinctive sound—small bells had been fastened to the bridle so the rider could descend on his prey with a sweet but sinister melody.

Sir Anthony tried to hasten Katharine along toward the protection of the gate, but his sixteen-year-old daughter was quick enough to move out of the way of his attempts to shield her. Katharine believed that it fell to her to protect her father from harm, and she stepped into the path.

Sir Anthony's man Baines reached for his weapon, an old-fashioned broadsword.

For a moment no one spoke.

"I wish you good evening," said Sir Gregory at last, with an abrupt courtesy.

His squire rode with him, a silent hulk named Cecil Rawes. Cecil was a new, taciturn arrival to Lord Pevensey's domain, and no one knew much about him. England was well supplied with rough hands looking for profitable employment and not above acts of violence. Cecil let his cloak hang open, windblown, and let the starlight gleam on the hilts of a rapier and a dagger with a brass knob.

"We are hale but cold," replied Sir Anthony with forced cheer. He kept a good grip on his walking stick, a knobby span of hazelwood that could serve as a defensive weapon.

"All the more reason to ask me in, then, to your hearth," said Sir Gregory, "so we can discuss business."

Sir Gregory Skere was a knight who had fought in Portugal against the Spanish, received a musket ball in the face, and retired to serve as a hired sword to whatever lord or lady would fill his purse with coin and his cup with malmsey, the sweet wine of his preference. Sir Gregory worked for Lord Pevensey, the most important landowner of the district. In the starlight Katharine could not make out what she knew was a battered visage under a cap that sported a single falcon feather.

"I should be glad to offer you bread and beef," said Sir Anthony, "but this evening's offering is not worthy of a man of your good name."

Katharine knew as well as her father that their pantry was reduced to rinds of cheese as hard as soap, and the darkest, most chewy bread, no food fit for a guest, and proof, furthermore, of their financial straits.

"Lord Pevensey," replied Sir Gregory, "in particular asked me to sit down with you and discuss most urgent business."

"We will be most grateful to his lordship," said Sir Anthony, "if he would be our guest on some night not many days from now, along with you and any of your friends."

Sir Anthony was a baronet, a minor but honorable noble rank. His estate had been in the Westing family since 1435, when a Westing named Robard wagered that his falcon could catch more pigeons than a hunting hawk owned by a Pevensey forebear.

Ever since Fairleigh and its land had been won by this sporting bet, the Pevensey family had fumed. Pevensey was an earl, and he owned orchards, grain mills, the fishing rights to major rivers, and every roof and chimney of several villages. A retinue of clerks and controllers was needed simply to accumulate his yearly rent.

Sir Anthony, in contrast, was the owner of unpretentious farmland, and was owed the services and rents of a few loyal folk. There was, however, the grand manor house of Fairleigh, complete with paved courtyards and a sprawl of chambers and fireplaces. The estate also featured a gatehouse, with an ancient gatekeeper, Sedgewin, who even now was opening the cross-timbered gates.

"We will speak business this very night," insisted Sir Gregory, "or my lord will be most displeased."

"My father is weary, Sir Gregory," interjected Katharine, "and fretful with his worries over an illness that plagues our stable, affecting even our broodmare."

If Sir Gregory had little regard for human beings, he nevertheless might wish to spare his horse contact with a croup or fever. This equine illness was a fiction—every last horse had been sold, and the stable stood quite empty.

"I saw your broodmare at market, Friday a week past, my lady," said Sir Gregory. "The one with the nick in the ear, the pretty bay. She's a good breeder, and as sporting as any female this countryside has produced, save, if I may say so, the young mistress of this place."

"No," said Baines, who had been trembling with ill-suppressed anger. "You may not say so, my lord, if you please, and you hear my master when he says that this is not a good night for visitors."

But as Baines pronounced this rugged attempt at courtesy, he made the mistake of gesturing with his sword, more to add meaning to his words than as a threat. Sir Gregory lifted a booted foot from his stirrup and kicked Baines hard in the chest.

The servingman went down, and Sir Gregory guided his steed forward with a quiet *cluck, cluck* sound. No horse would choose to put a hoof on a human body, which provided at best unsteady footing. But this horse had been trained, or at least had learned to accommodate his master. The horse placed a metal-shod hoof on Baines's chest as the man stirred, catching his breath.

"Please let me speak with you, Sir Anthony, inside where it is warm," said Sir Gregory with what was in him a great demonstration of diplomacy. "I would so regret," added the knight, "being forced to injure your man."

6

"LET ME SAY what we all know to be true, Sir Anthony," said Sir Gregory when they were all settled before the hearth.

"As you wish," answered Anthony. He added, with a dry laugh, "Although when a man sent by Lord Pevensey speaks of the truth, even the mountebank hides his coin."

"You wrong me, Sir Anthony," protested Sir Gregory. "I am not a bird hound, trained to leap at a whistle." Cecil sat in the shadows, firelight glinting off the brass pommel of his dagger as he took a long swallow of wine.

Anthony smiled and said nothing further for the moment. He was a tall, lean man with sandy hair. He was quick to take pleasure in life, and quick to grow concerned. He could hide his feelings from someone like Sir Gregory, who did not know him well and who was too vain—in Katharine's view—to sense another man's feelings in any event. Anthony could not hide his tensions or his happiness from his daughter, however, and she could see how anxious he was.

Their visitor leaned forward, with his elbows on the table. A maplewood cup of wine was beside him, the last of the best drink that Fairleigh had to offer. A fire was burning merrily in the grand fireplace—a great oak had fallen last winter in a gale, and firewood, if nothing else, was plentiful.

Sir Gregory gave a wondering glance at Katharine, who had joined the two men at the table. It was not entirely usual for women to confer with men, but with the death of Katharine's mother four years previously, Anthony had come to rely on Katharine's judgment regarding everything from whether he should wear a hood instead of a cap to whether the sheep—when there had been a flock—might be ready for shearing.

"My daughter," explained Anthony, "is my partner in commerce."

This phrase was calculated to carry weight—where business was concerned, age and sex stood aside for good judgment regarding money. While women entered life, and marriage, at a disadvantage, many a widow ran a prosperous business, and a bright husband might seek a wife with the capacity for balancing income and expense.

"What a prize," said Sir Gregory, "your daughter will be."

"She is a prize to me, as she was to her late mother," said Anthony. He added, perhaps foreseeing a discussion of marriage, "My daughter is not chattel."

Sir Gregory lifted a finger, as though to acknowledge

Anthony's remark without necessarily agreeing with him.

Baines entered the room at that moment, casting a baleful glance in Sir Gregory's direction. Baines was nearly the last of a committed staff of servants. Sedgewin the gatekeeper had stayed on, too, a man who had sailed to Naples as a youth and who now kept pots of dwarf oranges growing in tubs over the entrance to Fairleigh. Aside from Angus Deets, the cook, and his dimpled daughter, Molly, the once-renowned kitchen staff of Fairleigh had departed, including the ewer carriers and the bottler, the pantler and the scullery boy. Want of silver had forced Anthony to let even the most loyal and able of them go—and they were all faithful, warmhearted folk— with promises to hire them back when he could afford to.

Baines set a bowl of apples on the table, small, wormshot though they were—cider apples, most properly, and not sweet enough for ready eating.

"Will you be desiring anything else, sir?" Baines inquired, hovering protectively.

Anthony thanked Baines and said that there was nothing wanting. And in a way it was the truth. The dining chamber of Fairleigh Manor was a grand, pleasant room. The floor was covered with a mat of rushes woven with lavender and sage that even in its worn condition gave off a balmy perfume on this chilly night.

The hall was a treasury of fanciful wood carvings, doorposts and window frames ornamented with grinning imps and placid lions. The handles of the fireplace irons resembled hunting dogs of some hard-to-determine breed, and the tapestry on the wall depicted a griffin—an animal half eagle, half lion—sporting on a field of lily flowers.

Both Anthony and Katharine had a special fondness for this woven artwork. The tapestry had been crafted in the Loire and bought for a song by Anthony's father from Saint Bridget's Priory when it was disbanded, along with all the other abbeys and convents, during the reign of Henry VIII. Along with the family griffin banner, this would be one of the last items either of them would part with.

Sir Gregory waited until the door had shut behind the servant.

"You owe Lord Pevensey," said Sir Gregory, "several pounds of silver, a solemn debt which you promised to pay off completely by last Michaelmas, now nine months past."

Anthony sighed and gave a nod of agreement.

Gregory continued, "This sum was invested in a ship. The *Rosebriar*, Walter Loy captain, returning from the West Indies with a load of cinnamon bark and dyestuff. The shipment would be valuable enough in ordinary times, but thanks to the disrupted transport in recent seasons, the cargo is incalculably precious."

Sir Anthony gave a forced smile. "All true."

"But the ship," said Sir Gregory, taking a sip of his wine, "is more than two years out, and you have had no steady income all this while."

"The sea is an unsteady mistress," said Sir Anthony.

He had invested the loan in the ship, true enough, but he had also spent it on draining the stream near the windmill and repairing the stiles throughout Fairleigh. Furthermore, he had invested in books during his trips to the stalls of Saint Paul's in London: *Of the Heathens of Virginia and Their Practices*, and the weighty *The Healing of Wounds with the Grease of Fowls and Beasts, along with Other Marvels and Panaceas*, together with many pamphlets decrying Spanish lies and love of idolatry, and praising Sir Francis Drake for his bold raid on Cádiz. Sir Anthony loved to read.

"The ocean is hazardous," agreed Sir Gregory. "But where can you win greater honor?"

Katharine believed that Sir Gregory quietly envied seamen and wished he had chosen a mariner's life. "Lord Pevensey gave you a generous loan, and then there were those gambling debts you owe him from last Christmas."

"His lordship is a deft hand with dice," admitted Sir Anthony.

"Lord Pevensey, it may surprise you to learn, has purchased the debts you owe to tradesmen all over the south of England."

The scar on Sir Gregory's cheek resembled nothing so much, thought Katharine, as a third eye, closed tightly. He had a black short-cropped beard, with a mustache combed stylishly upward at the ends. He wore a large cuff at his wrist, folded back, as was the fashion, and held his hands together in a gesture that resembled prayerfulness without looking at all benevolent.

"Has he indeed?" asked Anthony after a brief silence.

He tried to sound unconcerned, but Katharine perceived the pinpricks of red that appeared in her father's cheeks and saw the just-visible tremor of anger.

"The debt you owe the thatcher, for instance," said Sir Gregory, "and the balance due the tiler. Not to mention the further debt you owe the goldsmith for that pretty little ring on Katharine's finger."

Katharine folded her hands and put them under the table. The gift had been for her last birthday, an extravagance that had embarrassed but pleased her, and Sir Anthony had prided himself on keeping the cottages of the Fairleigh tenants whitewashed and freshly thatched, for the benefit of the farmers and out of love for the family land.

Katharine sometimes wished she possessed a sibling to confide in, although in an imaginary sense she did have one. Katharine had been born just after her twin sister, Mary. Her twin had died after three days, as though, as her mother explained, "a sprite had stolen her breath." Katharine often felt this presence of Mary's companionship, a shadow so vivid it was alive. Surely such a sister would be helpful now, listening to this odious man with his broad Midlands accent.

"Adding these and other debts all together," said Sir Gregory, "I doubt that even a treasure ship of Peruvian gold would be enough to offset the debt you now owe Lord Pevensey."

"I have every faith," said Anthony, "that the *Rosebriar* will bring ample blessings from the West Indies."

"Until last week you did not even know," said Sir Gregory, "if the ship still swam the surface of the waves. But you have had good news."

"Indeed, very good news," agreed Anthony.

"The *Zephyr*," said Sir Gregory, "touched shore here with news that the *Rosebriar* was dismasted in a gale and is being refitted in the Azores, and you expect the ship with its sweet-smelling treasure to our waters in a matter of weeks." The Azores were Atlantic islands, nearly one thousand land miles west of Portugal, and celebrated as a safe haven for troubled ships.

"This is all as I understand it," responded Anthony. "Why do you make these happy tidings sound so meager?"

"Because, my friend," said Sir Gregory, "your debts to Lord Pevensey are so great that he will seek the Admiralty's permission to seize the ship and her cargo when she arrives in England."

Anthony sat in unhappy silence for a long moment. "This cannot be!"

"The document is being written up in Lord Pevensey's best ink," said Sir Gregory. "Cecil and I will carry the scroll to London."

"Why does Lord Pevensey," asked Katharine after

maintaining her own silence until now, "seek to ruin my father?"

"For profit," said Sir Gregory.

"He sent you to tell us this?" asked Katharine.

Sir Gregory said, "My lady, he did." The knight clasped his hands together thoughtfully. "You do know, Sir Anthony, that if you could tender me a gift, or even the promise of a gift, I would just as happily dispute on behalf of you and your daughter."

"I don't believe," responded Sir Anthony, with an air of pointed diplomacy, "that my daughter and I can afford your services."

"Perhaps not," replied Sir Gregory regretfully, and Katharine could see in his features a briefly younger, idealistic Sir Gregory, with hopes for his own destiny. "But fortune can surprise any of us."

Katharine wondered if she was the only living thing with the sense that she was attended by an absent twin. Perhaps, she sometimes thought, every mortal has a missing sibling, identical but separate, absent and yet never gone. This awareness of her faithful, long-vanished sister gave Katharine a sensitivity to the spoken word that made her feel all the more acute.

Even now, at the table with the two men, Katharine knew what was about to be offered. She asked nonetheless, if only to have her suspicions confirmed.

"What," she asked, "does Lord Pevensey really want?"

7

WHEN SIR GREGORY had finished his visit, he departed into the night, taking the shadowy Cecil with him.

Baines reappeared, clearing away the untouched apples. Anthony reached for one, and took a second, and Katharine realized how hungry she was, too, and joined him in emptying the plate of the slightly wizened fruit, the remains of last autumn's harvest.

"Sir," said Baines, "I'll not stand by and see you shamed, if you will forgive me for saying so."

"You were listening at the door, Baines," said Anthony in a tone of no great surprise.

"Truly, if I may say so, sir, the knight's voice carries," said Baines in a tone of ardent respect. Baines was a former seaman, and had a sailor's way of standing even now, his feet planted flat, prepared for the floor to begin to rise and fall. "I can collect young Carter and that spirited lad Percy, with your permission, and I'll arm them with pikes.

If Sir Gregory ever shows his face at Fairleigh again, he'll regret it."

Katharine was deeply moved by Baines's loyalty. His daughter, Eleanor, had been a playmate of hers, and a good friend. She had been married recently to a miller, and Katharine felt a certain good-hearted envy of Eleanor and her less ambitious, more peaceful existence.

"I WILL NOT have us ruined," said Anthony when father and daughter were alone, "and I will not have you married to Lord Pevensey."

That had been the offer, according to Sir Gregory—if she agreed to marry his lordship, the debt would be forgiven.

"Lord Pevensey is not such a brute of a man," offered Katharine, not meaning the words so much as experimenting with how they sounded.

They sounded terribly false.

"He is a greedy beast, as you know," said Anthony. "I should have seen these ill tidings before they arrived. I'll ride to London and bribe the Admiralty."

"With what in your purse, Father?"

Anthony limped up and down the room, his injury troubling him even more than before. The veteran stallion had failed to leap a hedge last Candlemas eve, and horse and rider had fallen heavily. Anthony had heard a bone or sinew snap, and now a painful ulcer on his ankle was slow to heal. The horse had survived and had been sold to meet Fairleigh's many expenses.

Anthony flung open the shutters and gazed out at the stormy darkness. Not all the windows in the fine house were glazed, but this window was leaded and glazed like any church window, and the rain beat down on the glass. "Katharine, do you want to marry that—that scheming weasel of a lord?"

"No," she said emphatically. "I believe I should have a favorable regard for the man I take as my husband."

"And so you should," agreed her father.

"I know that Lord Pevensey cheats at dice," she added, "and bribes cockfight stewards—and if the Devil came to Devonshire, he'd feel at home at Pevensey Hall."

"How does he cheat at dice?" asked her father.

"He pares them so they are off-weight—I saw him pocketing a little knife before you sat with him last Stephen's Day. I told you he cheated."

"Yes," he agreed thoughtfully, "you did."

"I don't like his lordship, and could love him only out of Christian charity, but I'll marry him tomorrow, Father, if it brings you peace."

"No, I'll outduel him before I allow you to share his bed."

"Fight him with a sword?"

"I studied the rapier and the dagger when I was young," said Anthony, "and I do believe that with Baines's help I could brush up my skills."

"We must consider a better plan."

She loved her father, and she had a deep respect for his resourcefulness. He had the energy to make a master swordsman of himself, if he put his mind to it, but she did not think any fair fight could defeat a devious, grasping soul like Lord Pevensey. Besides, her father's nagging wound would sometimes not allow him to walk with any comfort, much less engage in combat.

"I'll hire murderers," said her father.

"You are too gentle for crime, Father, except for the usual sort of half stealing from your creditors."

"He won't be seizing any ships," said Anthony, "with a new mouth cut out of his throat."

"You are not a great sinner, Father," said Katharine. "And to conspire to murder, you have to have a sinner's humor."

"Maybe I'll develop such a character," said Anthony.

"I pray not."

"The truth is, Katharine, that unless I think of a plan, either you will marry this grasping peer of the realm or we will be more destitute than two houseflies."

Despite her outward calm, Katharine felt bleak at their prospects. She was not one of those overly imaginative young women who thought wood pigeons spoke to them, but sometimes she did hear her name in the bells of the nearby Saint Simon's church, *Ka-thrine, Ka-thrine,* the first note higher than the second. Just now the sexton must be pulling on the bell, perhaps dislodging the swallows who liked to take up lodging in the belfry.

Hope soon, said the ungainly music as it spilled through the evening, *hope soon.*

"You will devise a way around this misfortune," she said encouragingly.

"Do you believe so?"

He was appealing, the way he needed to hear her express faith in him.

"Yes, you'll devise some cunning way out," she said.

"I think I will, too," he agreed with a laugh.

She joined him in quiet laughter. The truthful, objective alternative was too disheartening.

"By God," he said, listening to the weather outside. "This is a fierce tempest—I would not be on a ship tonight for all the gold in Christendom."

III
LAST BREATH

8

SHERWIN SANK into the cold sea.

He looked upward at the shifting, unsteady silken surface of the water—the life that he was leaving behind. The ship's keel was a heavy apparition, bearded with sea grass and barnacles, and the sea quaked, all that windy tumult quiet from beneath the waves. His last breath broke upward, carrying with it a fragment of prayer.

THE RESCUE began like an intrusion, an unwanted trespass into his beckoning quiet. Some presence broke the surface, and circles expanded outward across the muted starlight.

And he saw the hook, a descending, angry-looking grappling iron, searching downward on a long, uncoiling line like a serpent, a hunting creature whose touch would do him harm.

This time he seized the iron hook and hung on.

Soon Sherwin was out of the brine and into the windy

night. He was heaved up the side of the ship, banging against the vessel like a dangling wooden doll.

After being dragged over the gunwale, none too gently, he was stretched out upon the deck. Seamen nearby were manhandling the salvaged casks into the cargo hold using can hooks, short ropes with hooks at each end. Sherwin felt like a piece of salvage himself—of dubious value.

A broad, alert face gazed down into Sherwin's, with an expression like that of a man peering into a well. He had a wispy red beard and a nose that had evidently been broken at some time in the past. He wore a soldier's cap with a cock pheasant feather and a jaunty scarf of silk plush.

This individual lifted up a pale object, a fishlike shape Sherwin dimly recognized as his own hand. The warm fingers of this stranger tried to wrestle his father's signet ring off Sherwin's ring finger, and the endeavor succeeded after a long moment, the gold and garnet ring slipping down over his knuckle.

Sherwin gave a kick, coughed a fountain of salt water, and sat up.

"What nature of beast is he, Evenage?" called a voice from the quarterdeck.

"A gentleman, I reckon, Mr. Highbridge."

Strong arms carried Sherwin into a cabin belowdecks, where the same matter-of-fact folk stripped him of his linen shirt, and he was entirely naked.

The man called Evenage covered Sherwin with a thick wool blanket and handed him a metal cup of hot wine mixed with pepper and mustard. The beverage was so highly spiced Sherwin sneezed, nearly spilling it all.

He tried to ask a question, but the words would not come.

"Never mind the name of this ship, for now," said Evenage with a tone of friendly evasion. He had a pleasant voice. "Or the name of her captain. I am the sergeant of the vessel, here to pour as much of this hot wine down your throat as I am able."

A ship's sergeant was sometimes charged with serving as law officer aboard the ship, with the duties of locking up violent seamen, and—at times like this—investigating a new arrival.

"Sergeant Evenage, I thank you," said Sherwin through chattering teeth.

"The captain has a book of prayers," said the red-bearded man, "if you wish to read from it."

Sherwin was aware of the thanks he owed to divine mercy for so far sparing his life. He was not unusually pious, but neither was he a noted sinner. He did not like the sergeant's implication that he was in special need of divine intervention. "Why would I need the comfort of the captain's personal prayer book?"

"My good friend," said his companion, in a tone of regret, "I have to say that most men fished from such cold seas never survive the night."

9

AS HE LAY hugging the blanket around his trembling frame, Sherwin was visited by two other men.

One was a round, plump house cat of a man in a leather apron, who pressed his fingers into the pulse points on Sherwin's neck with an amiable but unconvinced manner, as though marveling that their new visitor was still among the living. Sherwin gathered that this man was either the ship's cook, estimating the time remaining before Sherwin could be served up to cannibals, or else the vessel's surgeon.

That this last impression was most likely was emphasized when a voice called, "The captain sends for you, Dr. Reynard," and this rotund, nearly silent man immediately reported to the upper deck.

The only other visitor to attend Sherwin's bed that night was an individual that Sherwin found a source of anxiety—a man who stayed well out of the swaying, unsteady lamplight and gazed upon Sherwin from the dark.

This silent spectator was dressed in a long black cloak with jet buttons, and a black cap that fit tightly over his head. He carried what looked like a golden circlet on a long ribbon around his neck.

From time to time he murmured some advice or question to Evenage or Dr. Reynard, and both men listened respectfully and answered briefly in low voices. The red-bearded sergeant always relaxed and sat down when the man in black left the quarters, and he stood in tense attention when the tall man's shadow fell across the cabin once again.

DESPITE HIS FATIGUE, his convulsive cold kept Sherwin awake all that night.

The lamp overhead swung with the movement of the ship. The seas continued to be heavy, judging by the circles and swivels of the light, and the shadows around Sherwin rocked and shifted. The *Patience* had been what was called a sweet ship, because years of carrying leaking casks of wine and spirits had mixed with the water in her ballast and caused her to have a pleasant smell.

This vessel, however, had a warship's ambience—the odor of gunpowder and iron. He also scented turpentine, made from the essence of evergreens, useful as a thinner for the thicker, blacker stone-pitch, and as a sealant for wood.

Another smell, too, permeated the soldiers' quarters, and Sherwin could identify the source only when Evenage crumbled a bit of black and yellow herb into a brass bowl at the end of a reed tube, and lit the leaves with a stick of smoldering cork.

"You'll want to empty out those ill humors, sir, as I'm sure you know," said Evenage, exhaling blue smoke. "This tobacco will bring you to life."

Sherwin had known tobacco smokers around Lincoln's Inn, men with a row of silver or brass pipe bowls, and a habit of gazing into the hearth while puffing, coughing, puffing, as though the herb gave men a bovine power of inner concentration even as it disgorged phlegm.

He had once read a printed broadside for sale in Paternoster Row, *The King of Trinidad's Daughter, Princess Tobacco*. While the aromatic plant had detractors, many authors praised its medicinal possibilities. Sherwin accepted the pipe from the sergeant's hands and fitted his lips over the mouthpiece. He inhaled, and he could feel the tobacco leaves burn hot in his fingers, and hear them expire in whispers.

He exploded in coughing.

And yet, within moments, a perplexing calm altered his concern just a little, as though he was a new, much wiser version of himself. He glimpsed empty bunks, and sea chests secured against the bulkhead. There was space in these efficiently arranged quarters for several men.

"Where are the other soldiers?" asked Sherwin, taking another curative pull on the reed. Again he coughed violently.

"They met with misfortune," said Evenage with a regretful sigh. "As fighting men now and again will." The sergeant wore a ruby ring on his left hand, and his buckles were silver. Sergeant Evenage grew even more serious when he added, "Watch your answers when First Officer Highbridge questions you. He holds your life in his hands."

"What nature of man is this Highbridge?" asked Sherwin.

The pipe had gone out, the fire extinguished, the herbs reduced to a black rind of crumbs. His strangely immobile tongue felt like bacon, smoked black and thick. Sherwin gave the instrument back to Evenage with his thanks.

"Peter Highbridge is an excellent first mate to the captain," said Evenage. "A good man. He knows the bobstay from the keel, I can tell you. But he's cunning, too, and quick to defend the ship."

A footstep on the deck above silenced the sergeant, and he lifted a finger to his lips.

10

THIN RAIN lanced downward through the opening as the tall man returned, brushing sea-foam from his long, dark mantle.

Doors and ports on the *Patience* had swung with noisy creaks, wooden complaints from every quarter of the vessel. The sound had been comforting to a traveler like Sherwin, who was essentially a landsman. The grunts and chuckles of the merchant ship had reminded him of the oak-pegged buildings of Chiswick and London, tall-timbered houses that gave gently under heavy feet and, by every estimation, could last for centuries.

This vessel was quiet, with oiled hinges, Sherwin surmised, and her planks sealed with oakum.

Highbridge stood over the bunk and gave Sherwin a smile.

"I see you are feeling better," said Highbridge. His tone was mild, but Sherwin had heard such mild men before, asking directions on their way to deliver death warrants.

"I am feeling more alive, sir," said Sherwin, "thanks to this sergeant's good efforts."

Highbridge considered Sherwin's simple, heartfelt answer as though Sherwin had quoted an axiom in Greek.

"He speaks like a young man of spirit, sir," said the sergeant. He added, "He could be a spy, it's true, but by my stars he is a worthy shipmate."

Sherwin felt pleased at this remark, and grateful.

But Highbridge seemed unimpressed. "Who are you?" he asked, looking hard at Sherwin.

Sherwin identified himself and his late father, and gave his hometown as Chiswick, by way of London.

"You sailed with Captain Pierson, as I guess," said Highbridge, "on the *Patience*."

"Sir, that is true," said Sherwin. He knew that his best strategy was to be honest but brief.

"What," asked his inquisitor, "were you doing on that ship?"

Sherwin gave a short account of his aspirations aboard the merchant vessel, and of his history of Captain Pierson's life, the notes for which were now lost, along with the untold secrets of the man's adventures. He concluded by changing the subject, and adding, "I want my signet ring returned to me if you will."

"We shall return your ring when it pleases our captain."

This was spoken without any courtesy or indeed any effort to soften the words. Sherwin was growing increasingly uneasy. Good manners were far more than a way of showing respect for social rank and importance. They also demonstrated compassion, and, in a world where legal torture was still sometimes applied, the absence of politeness could be the harbinger of serious trouble.

As though to make his sinister intentions clear, Highbridge added the further question "Why did the *Patience* sink?"

Sherwin's spirits stirred. "If you believe that I served Captain Pierson by setting his cargo alight, the Devil, sir, may take you."

"If you are a liar or a Spanish agent," said Highbridge, "we will bleed the truth out of you."

"Do you imagine that I am a sympathizer to Spain, bent on devastating the pleasures of Englishmen by destroying their brandy?"

Highbridge's smile was brief, but it was warmhearted. "We might wonder if the *Patience* carried some other, more ignitable cargo, in addition to wine spirits."

"Who captains this ship?" asked Sherwin, beginning to envision a letter of complaint about this ship and officer Highbridge to the Admiralty.

"Brandon Fletcher," said Highbridge, "is captain of the *Vixen*, by Her Majesty's leave."

Sherwin gathered the woolen blanket more tightly around his shoulders. This was not good tidings at all.

He had heard the stories about Brandon Fletcher, as had everyone else in England. Along with Francis Drake and Martin Frobisher, Fletcher was a seaman adventurer, although his reputation was more bloody than that of his competitors. He was known by name and by sight throughout Europe, his woodcut features appearing on pamphlets glorifying his exploits. Sherwin had studied these publications with keen interest.

While Drake had been the first Englishman to sail around the globe, and Frobisher had explored for a Northwest Passage to the Indies, Fletcher had spent a career robbing ships on the high seas, both merchant and military, and had been rumored to take an Englishman hostage at times, if his family could afford ransom. Fletcher had been active as a naval official when Sherwin's father began a career in law, and Sherwin prayed that Fletcher might recognize the greyhound symbol on the stolen signet ring as that of an old and valued acquaintance.

"Does Captain Fletcher," asked Sherwin, "believe that the *Patience* carried a hidden consignment of brimstone?"

"Captain Fletcher," said Highbridge with another fleeting smile, "believes what he chooses."

Brimstone was a major component of gunpowder, and in a country frantic to arm itself against foreign attack, the supply of the explosive powder was strained. The best sulfur was thought to come from the volcanic regions of the Mediterranean, and merchants were importing the flammable mineral while trying to keep the shipments out of the grasp of Spanish sympathizers.

Sherwin was increasingly angry that his honor could be

so starkly challenged, but he was aware, too, that on a vessel captained by a notorious brigand he might have few privileges and no pleasant prospects. He was deeply worried.

"If you will, please, sir," said Sherwin, "extend my compliments to Captain Fletcher, and ask him to spare me a moment of his time."

"Why," asked Highbridge, "would the captain find you worthy of an instant's conversation?"

"I can help to defend this ship," said Sherwin, trying to sound capable. "You appear to have lost a few fighting men, and I can handle a sword."

A warship usually had a small complement of soldiers on board. Men of money and good repute often funded voyages for adventure and profit, and were often quartered with these soldiers. When the ship found an enemy, a gentleman was considered another sword and was expected to join the battle.

"I can pay for the honor," added Sherwin.

Highbridge considered this.

"And I can pen a history of Captain Fletcher, as I was going to write one for Captain Pierson."

"Can you indeed?" said Highbridge, sounding doubtful but curious.

"Did you, by any chance, see my broadside on Drake's raid on Cádiz," asked Sherwin, "*The King of Spain Bearded in His Den and His Staunchest Ships Reduced to Kindling*?"

"The King of Spain rebuilt his fleet, and a hundred

more," said Highbridge, "and Drake merely made revenge inevitable, for all his swagger."

Feeling abashed, Sherwin nonetheless continued hopefully, "Mr. Highbridge, think of how I can further burnish the good name of Captain Fletcher with my pen."

There was a knock, and a ship's boy appeared, blond and thin, wearing a belt with a large brass buckle around his waist. The lad entered the lamplight, and it was evident that his face had been, in some recent event, peppered with small wounds.

"Compliments from the captain, Mr. Highbridge," said the lad. "The captain asks me to make certain that our new passenger is fed."

"See to it, Bartholomew," said Highbridge.

Then Highbridge did something that briefly puzzled Sherwin. He used the circlet of glass, a gold-rimmed lens, to examine Sherwin's hands. He surveyed the calluses on his right hand, and eyed the relatively smooth surface of his left.

Then Highbridge let the lens dangle and looked at Sherwin as a man might look at a bill nailed to a wall, a list of property being auctioned. Sherwin had never been gazed at so long, and with such quiet intensity.

But in conclusion Highbridge said, "You are no seaman, but you have been practicing with a sword." This time there was new promise in his smile. "And, in truth, there is the barest trace of ink on your fingers." He put his hand on Sherwin's shoulder and said, "Sergeant Evenage, I do believe that young Sherwin here will prove a worthy ship-mate indeed."

"I am not surprised to hear it, Mr. Highbridge," said the sergeant.

"We must see to it," added Highbridge, "that he does not die."

BARTHOLOMEW RETURNED with a wooden trencher of mutton and parsnips: fresh food, and delicious, much better than the frumenty—boiled wheat—and dried pike fish Sherwin had eaten on the *Patience*.

Sherwin had never before dined with such relish. Highbridge remained talking to Evenage about water in the hull, with the pumps being manned around the clock.

"We have no choice," confided Highbridge to the sergeant. "We must put in somewhere soon, or we will founder."

Sherwin realized, uneasily, that there was no fear in the first officer's voice, only the guarded attitude of a man who knew danger.

II

D ON'T LET HIGHBRIDGE frighten you," said the sergeant when he and Sherwin were alone. "He hates the Spanish and their secret agents more than he loves gold. He's a warrior, is our First Officer Highbridge, and a good-hearted man. We lost four soldiers against a prize ship off Bordeaux, and Highbridge and the captain took the losses hard."

A prize ship was a vessel that had been captured. Prize vessels were manned with as much of a crew as their privateer captors could spare, and sailed to a port to be ransacked and, very often, refitted under a new flag.

"Was this a ship that had been taken by the Spaniards?" asked Sherwin.

"No, sir, she was the *Santa Catalina*, manned by a crew of English privateers."

Sherwin felt mildly shocked, although he had heard rumors of such crimes. "Does Captain Fletcher steal from his countrymen?"

The sergeant laughed. "Sir, he does."

"And is it true that we are about to sink?"

Sherwin had hoped for a reassuring response, but instead the sergeant shook his head and said, "That, my friend, is beyond my power to foresee."

SHERWIN SLEPT.

At first his slumber was a cramped, shuddering semi-consciousness, from which he woke with terrified shocks, sure that he was about to drown. But gradually, as he woke once more to find Evenage polishing the brass and leather of his rapier sheath, or his large, unwieldy-looking wheel-lock pistol, Sherwin felt the lurch and toss of the ship to be reassuring enough to allow him to fall into a dreamless sleep.

HE DID NOT KNOW how many hours passed.

He woke at last to find Evenage gently shaking his shoulder, saying, "Be quick, sir—the captain will see you now."

Sherwin felt a tremor of helplessness pass through his spirits, huddled, as he was, naked in a blanket. And he was fearful at the prospects of holding a conversation with the notorious mariner.

"Sergeant," he protested, "I'm not prepared."

"Climb into these clothes, sir, if you will," said Evenage.

He indicated a neatly folded pair of serge breeches and a dark blue doublet. A pair of high boots stood rocking gently with the movement of the ship, as though a lively spirit inhabited the footwear.

"They belonged to my late friend Robin Fosque,"

explained Evenage, "who suffered a matchlock ball off Calais."

Sherwin felt some inner question as he fastened the belt around his waist, the mantle still faintly stained with the blood of a dead man. Would the spirit of his vanished shipmate be of assistance to him, or resent him for being alive? The boots were a little too roomy, but some gun wadding in the toe of each allowed for a snug fit.

Sherwin noted that Evenage did not offer him a sword.

THE HOUR was daylight, but the sky was filled with a cloud-cloaked, murky sunlight, the seas all around the ship white-capped and fuming.

Sergeant Evenage accompanied Sherwin, and Highbridge looked on from the ship's waist, the space just before the quarterdeck, in a place partly sheltered from the elements. Each step took a long heartbeat, and Sherwin kept his eyes downcast—in his uneasiness he did not want to meet the gaze of the famous privateer.

Until at last he had no choice.

CAPTAIN FLETCHER was a gray-haired, red-cheeked man with sharp, slate-blue eyes and a way of looking away before he spoke.

There was, it was true, much to observe all around.

The seas were boiling with further tempest, and the wind howled through the tightly furled sails. Men worked their way along the ship using handlines, gripping tightly as water seethed over the deck. The captain stood to one side of the quarterdeck, clinging to the rail with casual ease. The ship slanted heavily to starboard as she coursed through the white water.

To make matters more dramatic, in Sherwin's view, the vessel was approaching the rocky surf and chalky outcroppings of what Sherwin took to be the Devonshire coastline, with a strong wind pushing her and the captain making no effort, for the moment, to escape a violent encounter with the impending land.

Sherwin clung to the rail in an attempt to imitate the captain's nonchalance. The unfamiliar mantle Sherwin had donned was stout wool, rich with natural oil, and it kept off the rain, although his boots and breeches were already damp from the foam lashing the air.

Sherwin judged the *Vixen*'s length to be some ninety feet, and estimated her to be twenty feet across at her widest point. She was much smaller than many of the Spanish warships famous throughout the world, but, with her modest dimensions, she was a typical English fighting ship. He knew, further, that with four or five decks below, a powder magazine, and a complement of arms, she was able to feed, arm, and deploy herself in no mean way. Well fewer than a hundred men would be enough to sail her around the world, if the captain desired such an endeavor.

"Is it true, as Highbridge reports," asked the captain at last, "that you were going to write a history of that plodding merchant mariner Captain Pierson?"

Sherwin stiffened with this affront to the good name of

his late friend and master. "I was, sir, already at work with my pen, and I found Captain Pierson's character to be adventuresome and admirable."

"I have encountered cheddar with more character than Pierson," said Captain Fletcher, adding, as one does of the dead, "God grant him peace."

"Captain Pierson's career took him to Africa and the West Indies," Sherwin added, bristling inwardly at the lack of respect shown to his deceased mentor. "He had transported silks, velvet, pig iron, and silver reals in his day, and knew all the tactics of trading in the East."

"Did he?" queried Fletcher dryly.

"Pierson was a hard man to cheat," said Sherwin. "He knew the Turkish trick of dyeing silk with a pigment easily washed off so that it resembles indigo but is one-tenth the value."

"Captain Pierson," said Fletcher with an ironic smile, "must have been a phenomenon of marketing shrewdness."

"Sir," said Sherwin, "if you will forgive me, I believe he was."

"What were you going to call these weighty volumes of Pierson's blazing history? *A Hercules for Our Own Era: Danger and Death Surmounted to Bring Taffeta to the Strand*?"

Despite himself, Sherwin felt a flicker of amusement. "That title has a certain charm, sir, if only I had ink to write it down."

"Well, you'll find my own history astonishing and deserving of the highest praise."

"Perhaps, sir, you may be right."

"Perhaps? There can be no doubt. I will dazzle and edify you. My life has been more dramatic than that of the bantam rooster Drake, with his puffed-up reputation, and far more salty than Frobisher's, that dour hulk. As for Captain Hawkins, the man was a slave trader, and I've never trafficked in humans."

"No doubt your history will be wonderful to write and even more delightful to read," Sherwin allowed.

"The matter is settled, then," said Captain Fletcher. "You will write the history of my life. Can you rhyme?"

"Sir?"

"Can you write rhymes, like those declamations one hears from the stage, Hector sword-to-sword with Achilles, all in couplets?"

Seamen, explorers, and military men vied with each other to complete the stories of their exploits. Some, like the impressive Walter Raleigh, were beginning to pen their own chapters, but others needed a co-author with access to a vigorous muse.

"I had in mind a prose work, sir," said Sherwin, still unwilling to completely commit his talents to the service of this notorious seaman.

"That will do, I suppose, if you salt and sugar it well." He sounded downcast, however, and in need of encouragement.

Sherwin felt inspired to improvise.

"But were some tale of yours to live through time,
You should live in it first, rhyme or no rhyme."

Sherwin spun this in the moment, and hoped the awkward couplet would serve to satisfy the prideful captain that poetry was not his gift.

"You have a degree of aptitude," said Fletcher, "but you lack proper encouragement—and spirited material."

"I hope for the muse's attendance," said Sherwin, feeling mild irritation despite his own modest estimation of his poetic skills, "every time that I dip my quill."

"You keep on with me, and mark me as I speak," said Fletcher. "I'll inspire your powers, and we'll have the world forget these trifling privateers, my competitors, in a play composed of poetry."

"I'll need paper," said Sherwin, feeling enthusiasm at the prospect of exciting work, and undeniable fame, "and a decent goose quill—no doubt I can find some tonight in Southampton."

"Where?" asked the captain, with an absent air.

"Surely," said Sherwin, "with a following wind like this, we'll be in harbor by nightfall."

"Oh, no," replied the captain with a laugh. "There are so many good reasons why we mustn't show our necks in any harbor. And our course is well west of the usual naval ports in any event."

"Are we heading toward some secret anchorage?" Sherwin asked with what he realized sounded like naïve speculation.

Smugglers and privateers often concealed their ships in along the rugged Devonshire and Cornwall coastline, but the practice could be dangerous. While there were many safe coves, there were also sandbars notorious enough to have names like Dragon's Reach and Red Graze. These menaces to shipping arose and vanished over the seasons, and moved from place to place, and even the currents were hard to predict.

The captain found Sherwin's question amusing, it seemed by his smile, and did not answer directly. "You'll need some servant, I believe, someone to your keep your boots on the proper feet. Young Bartholomew Ingby was training with Master Gunner Aiken, but I believe he'll be better suited to keeping you in one piece."

"Sir, you are too kind."

"I knew your father," the captain said. "Highbridge told me of your recent sorrow, and you have my condolences." The captain reached into his mantle. He withdrew the signet ring. He did not release the ring, but held it with a tender yet covetous air, admiring the design.

"Do you agree, my literate friend," asked the captain, "to pen my history?"

This was a simple question, but Sherwin felt that his future—his breathing, waking living in the months or years to come—depended on his response.

"Captain, I do."

Fletcher placed the ring in Sherwin's hand.

Sherwin felt gratitude and relief.

But he also felt increasingly alarmed as the wind stayed strong from the south, driving the *Vixen* toward the stewing surf of the shore.

12

T HE BREAKERS DREW NEAR, along with the cliffs, with their weather-swept vegetation, and a smell, even with the wind against them, of fertile lowland and cattle, grassland and mud.

There was a tug at Sherwin's sleeve, and the blond boy with the sprinkle of wounds across his features was saying, "Sir, the captain says you will need this."

Sherwin thankfully accepted a handsome rapier, sheathed in silver-chased leather.

"I thank you, Bartholomew," said Sherwin.

"Don't fasten the sword on yet, sir, if it please you," said Bartholomew. "All hands will need to help work the ship."

Sherwin thanked him again, and added, in a tone of kind curiosity, "Were you injured in the encounter with the *Santa Catalina*?"

"No, sir, before that we encountered a rich Spanish ship, off the Algarve, on her outward voyage, filled with sheep and chickens."

That, thought Sherwin, explained the meal he had most recently eaten.

"We were beating to windward to close in on her, sir, and a culverin charge struck me in the face."

"How was it you survived?"

"The gun was filled with nails and scrap iron, sir, but we were almost out of range and it only kissed me."

Sherwin gave a low whistle of appreciative amazement. "Bartholomew, you were very lucky."

"That's why I believe, sir," came the reply, "the captain wants us together."

"Because you might bring me luck?"

"Because we are both lucky, sir, to be alive."

"Or unlucky enough," Sherwin suggested, "to have experienced all-but-mortal calamity."

"Or that, too, sir. I think the captain wants to discover which."

SAILORS ON THE *PATIENCE* had been clothed in slop-breeches of no great quality, but the crew of Fletcher's ship wore the finest richly dyed fustian, and every buckle was silver, or silver plate, and brightly polished.

The *Vixen*'s boatswain was a quick, slight man named Tom Lockwood, with a short yellow beard and a way of being able to be on one side of the ship and then the other with a flea's alacrity. The boatswain was in charge of the sails and the rigging, and much of what a person saw when he gazed around above decks. He called seamen to their various duties and, after the captain and the first mate, the boatswain was the most able mariner on the ship.

Lockwood responded to Highbridge's quietly voiced commands with a short signal on his boatswain's call, a brass pipe with a shrill but pleasing sound.

Lockwood must have noticed the apprehensive look in Sherwin's eye. "We'll sail her across meadow and field, all the way to Exeter, sir," he said with a laugh, "and be there by candle-time."

"I have no doubt," said Sherwin, hanging on to the port gunwale in anticipation of what he expected to be a ferocious collision with the shore.

The boatswain's mate was a man named Randall Nittany, with blue eyes so keen and a gaze so steady he gave the impression of being able to see through several fathoms at a glance. He was appointed to smell the ground, as the boatswain put it—using a weighted line to plumb the water and report how rapidly the sea bottom was rising to meet the keel.

THE *VIXEN* surged toward the shore, and through either luck or astuteness she avoided the foam-covered rocks on either side of the modest inlet. She was close to the shadow of a high embankment of earth before her keel kissed the bottom. The masts and the rigging shook, timbers groaned, and Sherwin nearly lost his footing.

The captain gave a nod to Highbridge, and the dark-mantled first mate spoke to the boatswain. The boatswain's call pronounced a staccato message, and sailors responded at once, several men leaping over the side and using ropes to pull the ship very much higher onto the beach, aided by the flood tide and the surging gale.

THERE WAS LITTLE obvious outward reaction to the presence of a new shipmate.

Sherwin pulled, hand over hand, with his novel companions, and there was a quality of cheerful teamwork to the effort. But there was a quality of suspicion in the sideways glances of a few of the seamen, too, as Sherwin betrayed some clumsiness at hauling on the line.

Sherwin believed that he understood why.

In a world of instant death, the idea of luck was more essential to a mariner than to a townsman. Sherwin and Bartholomew were both questionable, having survived their respective misfortunes. They might be the best sort of shipmates to have on board, blessed with an additional power to survive. Or they might be just the opposite, the kind that attracted trouble.

Securing the ship upon the shingle and sand of the beach was a matter of careening her, and that was accomplished by men pulling on the rope attached to the masts and hauling with a unified effort. Sherwin joined in, as did everyone but the captain, who stumped along the shore, with his gaze to seaward, and Highbridge, who stood with one hand on the ship's prow like a man calming a nervous mare.

The ship very gradually heeled over.

The task was achieved to the singsong *heave, oh,* with a firm emphasis on the *oh.* The ship took on her new position as required, leaning on her side, and although the masts bobbed forlornly and the ratlines went slack on the downward side and taut on the other, the ship appeared sturdy enough to weather the indignity of exposing the barnacles and sea growth of her keel.

THERE WAS A FURTHER FORMALITY that did much to ease what might have been the lingering doubts of a few of Sherwin's new shipmates.

Highbridge opened a large, leather-bound book, placed it out of the wind, in the shadow of the ship, and anchored the pages with stones from the shingle-strewn beach.

The first mate was quietly reserved, as before, and he dipped a quill into an inkhorn with a grave manner. He said, "If you will write your name, sir, alongside all of ours."

By signing the ship's articles, Sherwin knew, and by joining the vessel's company, he was entitling himself to share in a percentage, however small his fraction, of her earnings. He was also committing himself to profit by the prizes taken by a captain of no great virtue, a man who did not balk at robbing his own countrymen. And Sherwin could foresee a cloudy future, his reputation tainted.

But he could also see himself becoming the confidant of a captain who knew more of the world than nearly any other mortal. Sherwin had already agreed to write this man's story, a tale any person in the world would be sure to find fascinating.

And even more exciting, in Sherwin's view, he saw the possibility of a war against Spain, with Captain Fletcher playing an essential role, and Sherwin there to earn his portion of renown.

Besides all that, there was money to be won.

Sherwin was aware that he was being watched as he took the quill in hand. He read the articles, which had been penned with a Greenwich clerk's steady hand. He would receive his share, like the other officers of the ship, of one-twentieth of her prizes—far more than an able seaman, and as much as the surgeon.

The final phrase caught his eye: *God save and defend Her Majesty.*

Sherwin signed willingly, and with a thrill, believing that with the squeaking of the quill against the broad page he was already embarking on the defense of his country.

IV

HAZARD AND
DEATH

13

THE RAIN HAD CEASED, and the sun made inroads into the overcast clouds. The shore resembled bread that had been broken and scattered, with some round loaves remaining intact and others crumbled into chunks of brown crust.

Sherwin felt dismay at the manner in which the vessel, so stalwart at sea, appeared utterly helpless on shore. She was, even so, an impressive ship. The *Vixen* was a type of vessel made popular by Fletcher's rival privateer John Hawkins, who had found that the old-fashioned carracks with their towering forecastles were less seaworthy than a ship with more modest lines. Like most such galleons, the *Vixen* had three masts, square-rigged on her fore- and mainmast, with her mizzen mast, nearest her stern, rigged for a slanting sail.

Sherwin took the opportunity to look into the gaze of her figurehead, the carved image of a woman with blue eyes and black hair, one arm sweeping across her breast in modesty or self-defense. This hand held two arrows, and the figure's outlines were well coated with paint, down to the gilded points of the arrowheads. Sherwin had rarely seen a statue of any kind—the churches had been cleansed of the images of saints during the religious up-heaval well before Sherwin's childhood, and looking at this larger-than-life image stirred his deepest deference.

Captain Fletcher crunched across the shore to join Sherwin gazing at the carved figure, who in her nearly horizontal position looked like a matron whose dignity was nearly under doubt.

"I had this ship shadow-built to my design, some twenty years past," said Fletcher. *Shadow-built* meant that no drawn plan had been used, only the exacting vision of the builder.

Sherwin knew something of boatwrights, having grown up around the wherries and scull-boats of the river Thames. The construction, out of a single vision, of a ship like the *Vixen* struck Sherwin as nothing short of mar-velous.

"Is the ship as fine as you had hoped?" Sherwin asked.

"She is the very echo of my dream," said the captain, gazing at the vessel with an air of affectionate pride. "When it came to this stalwart maiden, the figurehead, the carver followed my orders, but he wanted her to clasp a cross." He gave the wooden figure a caress. "He was an older man with, I think, antiquated religious sympathies. I thought arrows were more fitting."

The captain added, without pause, or change of tone, "We are being watched."

A HEAVILY CLOAKED FIGURE was observing the ship from the summit of the cliff, a young woman, Sherwin judged, with light brown hair.

"I am not well pleased by having a witness," said Captain Fletcher, "especially when my pretty ship is lying on her beams. I hope to be at sea again by midnight, after the next flood tide. Until then a visit by a port constable or one of his tipstaves would be unwelcome." Tipstaves were a constable's attendants, notorious for putting their staves to rough use.

"Is concealment so very important?" asked Sherwin.

"We need secrecy while we heal. Do you see this wound," added the captain, "there below the waterline?"

The captain indicated a tear-shaped gash below the gunports, like a long single claw mark ending in a round hole. As matter-of-fact as the wound was, exposed to the daylight, Sherwin's breath caught at the sight, the secret wound looking small but mortal.

"Made by a Spanish gun firing ten-pound shot," said the captain. "It pains me to see such an injury. The carpenter and his mate will have her mended, under my care, but we've been taking on water, and with the trouble to come we can't let the damage go untended. She'll be seaworthy again by nightfall, but until then we are vulnerable."

"What," Sherwin found himself asking, hoping that he already knew the answer, "is the trouble that is bound to come?"

"A great fleet, as men describe it," said the captain. "The largest navy ever to set sail, if the drain of shipwrights from Porto to Parma, from what I hear, is any evidence. This would be the greatest sea force of all time—a historic armada—if the reports are true."

To hear the possibility so described gave Sherwin a quiet thrill—and a surprising degree of dread, too.

"And you'll want the *Vixen* to be fit so you can join the battle," said Sherwin, sure that he understood the captain's meaning.

"What I hope to be, when the fury begins," responded the captain, "is as far away as possible."

"We are not, I hope, a white-livered ship," said Sherwin. It would not be polite or even wise to say *cowardly*.

"Do you think cowardice has any meaning for me," said the captain, "or courage, for that matter? While the entire world is gathered to spoil the sea with blood, we'll slip north to pluck a few ocean geese off Bristol, or Liverpool." He stopped to consider his remarks, and then he added, "Although I would enjoy getting my hooks into a Spanish prize."

Highbridge had joined the two of them, and listened to the captain's comments with a keen look in his eye, although he made no effort to join in the conversation.

For his part, Sherwin was badly surprised to hear the

captain's blithe dismissal of defending his country. And this surprising outlook certainly dashed Sherwin's enthusiasm at putting his life into the captain's hands.

Sherwin recovered his good humor. He allowed himself to chuckle. "I do not believe you, sir, if you will forgive me. If the need arises, you will be as stalwart as any of the Queen's subjects—and more fervent, I am sure."

He knew that some men pretended to be foolish to hide their actual cunning, or to make themselves agreeable. Other men pretended to be kind in order to mask their cruelty. Captain Fletcher was surely hiding an ardent, if perhaps discomfiting, love of his country by pretending to be purely interested in personal gain.

"Why, then, good Sherwin," replied the captain, "I hope no war comes. Otherwise, you will find me very disappointing."

Sherwin was about to express further good-natured skepticism when the captain interjected. "Oh, damn me—she has vanished."

The womanly figure was no longer on the cliff.

"I was going to invite her down so I could tell her lies about who we are and what we are doing." The captain added, "It has been many a month since I spoke to a lady."

Captain Fletcher set a lookout on the cliff, the sharp-eyed Nittany, and he also sent three groups off to forage in different directions. Sherwin and Bartholomew were assigned to a group composed of Sergeant Evenage and a seaman named Giles Tryce.

BEFORE SHERWIN'S TEAM of foragers departed, Highbridge beckoned silently to Sherwin.

The first mate had a wooden box under his arm. He set
the container down on the stony beach and pried it open.

"I would be most pleased," said Highbridge, "if you carried this."

Highbridge gave Sherwin a dag—a heavy, large-bore
pistol.

It was a sturdy weapon, made of stag ivory and iron,
decorated with pretty silver patterns. The firearm was very
much like the one Evenage had been cleaning earlier,
except even more beautiful.

"This belongs to me," said Highbridge. "I am loaning it
to you, during the duration of your stay aboard the *Vixen*.
The sight of such arms impresses shipmates and villagers
alike."

Sherwin stammered his thanks. He added, "I don't
know the art of using such weapons."

There was a twinkle in Highbridge's eye, and it was not
the first time that Sherwin believed that his initial, severe
impression of this man had been entirely wrong.

"Bartholomew," said Highbridge, "will show you how
the weapon works."

"I will be most grateful."

"And you will," continued Highbridge, "in exchange for
the use of this weapon, encourage the captain to allow you
to use it against the Spanish."

This assertion was a surprise, and helped to explain the officer's generosity. He was seeking an ally.

"Sir," said Sherwin, "I shall do my best."

"Good man," said Highbridge with a smile.

LATER, as Sherwin started along the path leading up the face of the cliff, he fully appreciated the trust Highbridge had shown in him.

An insistent, quiet inner voice was urging him toward freedom.

As he set eyes on the fine expanse of land from the top of the cliff, Sherwin was teased by the realization that he could run off across the fields of this farmland and never return. No admiralty court would punish Sherwin for escaping after his signature had been entered into a contract with a pirate. Such coerced agreements were common—merchant captains had signed away their ships, under threat, only to recant once they reached a safe harbor.

But Highbridge sought an alliance with Sherwin in persuading the captain to take part in the impending warfare.

That should prove easy enough, thought Sherwin, a spring in his step.

After all, what would the looming conflict be, if not a grand adventure?

14

FROM THE CLIFFTOP the *Vixen* looked not help-less so much as lost to the effects of a night's carous-ing.

Her rigging sagged drunkenly, and the sailors settled, warming their hands around a fire or spreading their clothing and other belongings out on the sand to be dried by the waxing sunlight. They looked like stumpy-legged harvesters, foreshortened by the altitude from which he viewed them, and it seemed pure folly to Sherwin that these men would trust their lives to that cracked walnut of a vessel, being slowly left behind by the ebbing tide.

The mantled young woman was nowhere to be seen, but what was entirely visible was a green field and a road rutted by cart wheels, with oaks and a blue sky breaking through the clouds. The wind was turning serene, and Sherwin felt again the joy of arrival in a magnificent location.

The hedges were in full flower, or just past, with briar berries already formed, green and covert among the bristly leaves. Bees fumbled and found blossoms, and a wagtail perched at the edge of a puddle and gave a toss of its tail feathers like a finger beckoning, urging Sherwin forward.

Sherwin was happy and excited. He felt his future flower with exceptional opportunities. Furthermore, if he encountered the young woman, and if she saw fit to exchange pleasantries, Sherwin believed that his appearance would not displease. While soldiers and gentlemen wore nothing like a uniform garment, Sherwin was dressed much like the sergeant, who was a far from shabby figure.

Sherwin wore tall boots that folded down below the knee, and a dark blue doublet, with a cup-hilted rapier swinging at his side. Bartholomew had used a solution of vinegar and brine to further diminish the stains of blood on the mantle. Most pleasing of all was the leather-and-felt hat, which sported the feather of a cock pheasant. The late Robin Fosque had taken heed of his appearance, and Sherwin was in his debt.

As yet Sherwin had seen no humans other than his companions, although a large white horse looked up from a patch of harebells and gave his head a toss—curious, Sherwin had to believe, as to why the visitors did not stop to climb over the stile and come toward him with gifts of hay or apples.

Now that he was no longer on the ship, Sherwin could smell himself and his shipmates, a strong odor of tar and sweat, sharpened by salt water, rising from the fabric of his garments.

"Will you show me how to load the pistol with a bullet?" asked Sherwin.

Bartholomew's undertakings, as an attendant to a gentleman, included carrying the powder holder, a large ox horn that was embellished with brass fittings, an iron nozzle, and a stout leather strap. He accepted the weapon itself from Sherwin's hands, and as they walked he used the ramrod to probe the barrel.

Then he sat beside the road and took no small amount of time loading the firearm.

At last he stood again. "She holds a charge ready," he announced, and handed the weapon back to his master. He explained the firing of the weapon, and added, "Let us hope, sir, your life never depends on this."

Sherwin thrust the pistol through his belt as they continued to make their way, considerably in the rear of the sergeant and Tryce.

"What keeps the lead shot and the gunpowder from drooling out the end of the barrel?" asked Sherwin.

"Gun wadding," said Bartholomew. "And fortune."

"How long have you sailed on the *Vixen*?" asked Sherwin.

"Not four months," said Bartholomew. "I joined her in Calais. Sir, my master was imprisoned." He pronounced the town's name *Cal-ass*.

"What sort of duties did you perform for your master?"

"Sir, I was a toad-eater."

"A toady?" asked Sherwin in surprise.

"My master was the mountebank John Pourbonne. He was renowned for his sleight-of-hand marvels, and among these, sir, he had the power to make creatures vanish."

The toad, more than other amphibians, was considered to be poisonous. A toad-eater's job was to hide the noxious creature while the magician showed that nowhere—not up this sleeve or even under this cap—was the vanished toad. "Madam, could it be the toad is here?" the magician would say, tickling a buxom goodwife under her ribs to a chorus of giggles.

"My master and I," continued Bartholomew, "earned pennies by the bushel in Dover and Portsmouth, but he wanted a brighter future. He took a French name, and we thrived for a time."

Sherwin had seen mountebanks on market day throughout his childhood. He liked them, but would not trust one. He suspected they were quick-handed thieves at heart, and they sold elixirs that were thought to inspire love, conquer age, and cure poor vision.

"Do they piss?" Sherwin could not help but asking. "The toads, while in your mouth?"

"Our toad was educated," said Bartholomew.

Sherwin walked for a while, considering.

"How," he asked at last, "do you educate a toad?"

"Dry him out," said Bartholomew.

"Do you prefer Captain Fletcher," asked Sherwin, "to your imprisoned master John Pourbonne?"

"John once made me hide a scorpion, sir," said Bartholomew, "under my tongue. Captain Fletcher has made no such command."

SHERWIN AND BARTHOLOMEW had hurried up by then to reach the sergeant and Tryce, and as they passed a puddle Sherwin took a moment to examine his reflection.

"As worthy as a magpie," snorted Tryce, noticing Sherwin's momentary indulgence in vanity, "like most gentlefolk."

"Ah, Tryce," chided the sergeant. "By my faith, you've all manners of mange."

The four of them approached a cottage not far from the sea cliff, a whitewashed dwelling with a broad door, heavily shuttered windows, and a thatched roof. Judging by the sharp smell in the air, there were pigs nearby.

"I don't know anything about swine," said Tryce. "I imagine you stick a pig with a blade and it dies like any animal."

"We aren't going to steal livestock," said Sherwin.

"I doubt we are not," said Tryce with an enigmatic smile.

Tryce was the sort of man Sherwin had seen rolling casks into the wine warehouses along the London docks, and lounging outside Southside alehouses, scarred and suntanned, with an air of dangerous good nature. Sherwin relished the chance to know one of these men better.

The four of them paused beside a head-high wall of whitewashed stone, surmounted by jagged flint rocks, a sharp margin along the tip of the barrier to discourage men like Tryce. Dogs not far away began to bark, the knowledgeable, communicative baying of animals fit for duty. A goose joined in, from somewhere unseen, a loud, brazen noise.

"I'll pay for the pig myself when we find one," said Sherwin.

"With what?" asked Tryce.

Sherwin realized that, when it came to ready money, he had neither gold nor silver, all of his possessions having gone down with the *Patience*.

"I'll reimburse you any debt," said Sherwin, "when I am able to draw on my late father's accounts in London. Or when I have been paid my share of the captain's prizes."

"I don't owe money," said Tryce, "and I don't credit any debts, either."

The lack of courteous, softening interjections was pronounced in Tryce's manner of speaking, no *By my guess* and certainly no attempt to call Sherwin *sir*, as would have been proper.

"I'm not going to meander the countryside," said Sherwin, "taking advantage of innocent farmers."

"That's what you're doing, though," answered Tryce, "isn't it?"

Tryce had adopted a tone of challenge, and Sherwin acknowledged to himself that his new companion would make a tough opponent. He was a big man, as sailors go, with broad shoulders and the rolling gait of a man used to the deck shifting under his stride. He had a broad-bladed sword in a worn scabbard, and a salt-stained, bruise-blue knit cap on his head, the end dangling over his ear.

"Best we leave the actual thievery to Tryce, sir," advised Sergeant Evenage. "He's a rough-cut sort, as you can see, and he can't easily tell right from not-right-at-all, if you catch my meaning."

Bartholomew put his hand on Sherwin's arm and gave a nod of agreement.

"But what difference does it make," protested Sherwin, "if we end up dining on a sow that Tryce has stuck with a knife?"

"I am a soldier, sir," said Evenage, "and not altogether accustomed to some of the ways of Captain Fletcher's men myself."

"But you profit from their plunder, I can easily imagine," said Sherwin.

He turned to advise Tryce to stay where he was.

But it was too late.

TRYCE HAD LEAPED over the white wall, and judging by the sounds of sloppy footsteps, he was making his way through a sty.

The musical, shrill gutturals of piglets greeted his entrance among them, and Tryce could be heard more than once calling "Hoi, you," as—judging by the sounds— he groped and stumbled into puddles.

"Sir," cried Bartholomew, "take care."

Sherwin climbed to the top of the wall, and overlooked a catastrophe.

15

TRYCE WAS RUNNING fast, back toward Sherwin, pursued by a very large white-and-brown pig.

Tryce stumbled and the sow was upon him.

Sherwin leaped from his uncomfortable perch on the wall and was thankful for his tall boots, which allowed him to wade with a certain dignity and alacrity through the muck.

The sow had torn a long slash into Tryce's breeches and drawn blood as Sherwin hurried to help his companion. Breed sows, although not tusked or muscled as heavily as boars, were equipped to defend their young. As Tryce bawled for the help of Heaven, this huge, heavy creature was on him, trying to roll the trespasser onto his back where she could rip him open.

Sherwin had enjoyed a variety of acquaintances along the river Thames in Chiswick. Reed-gatherers and plowmen, swineherds and squires took the time to wish each other good day. Sherwin had passed a piggery nearly every summer afternoon on his way to fish for smelt in the river-island shallows, and he had enough knowledge of swine temperament to realize what danger Tryce was in, and to know exactly what had to be done.

He drew his rapier.

ASIDE FROM DRAWING the sword briefly on board the ship, Sherwin had never put this blade to even experimental use before now. This was not a city dweller's slender length of steel but a thicker, shorter, more deadly-looking weapon, made for use on a warship.

He knew, however, that stabbing the attacking sow with this still-unfamiliar sword could well prove fatal to the pig, but would do little to save Tryce before she succumbed.

Using the hilt of his sword, Sherwin struck the sow on the flat of her nose. He struck her very hard, and on the third clout the sow redirected the gaze from her small, dark eyes right at Sherwin.

"Fly, Tryce, fly," came the sergeant's urging from the top of the wall, and Tryce lost no time in plucking himself out of the muck, where a Tryce-shaped declivity remained, filling slowly with groundwater. He bounded, stride by stride, and threw himself over the wall.

Several more strong blows against the wet snout of the sow were necessary to allow Sherwin space to back slowly, eyes on his adversary. The sow struck and retreated, backing off and surging forward, using her bulk and momentum as a battering ram against Sherwin's boots, and nearly succeeding in knocking him down. As absurd as his situation was, and as worthy as it might be to provide amusement over beer for years to come, Sherwin was fully aware that the pig could take his life.

He continued to keep his sword in hand and to back up with slow, steady steps until he reached the wall, where Sergeant Evenage gave him a hand up, over the jagged flint, and out into the peaceful security of the road.

"Did you kill her?" was Tryce's first question.

"Tryce, I spared the pig's life," said Sherwin.

"I am unseamed, nearly, by a piggery bitch," retorted Tryce, "and you grant her mercy!"

"What our friend is trying to offer, sir," said the sergeant with an approving smile toward Sherwin, "is his thanks for your efforts."

"I'll thank him no thanks," spat Tryce.

But then they all fell silent.

THEY WERE NOT ALONE.

Two men in high-gartered, mud-flecked leggings and farmers' beige tunics approached from the direction of the cottage. In their hands they carried farming implements that could be put to easy use as weapons.

The taller of the two carried a billhook, a long device, recently sharpened, Sherwin thought, judging by the gleam of the heavy iron hook-and-blade. The younger, stouter man brought a mower's scythe, a large one, made for felling grain during harvest, and for swiftly clearing briars during the spring's first toil.

The men were joined by dogs, three of them, good-sized, bristling animals with white teeth. The dogs were restrained by spoken commands as quiet and peremptory as any aboard the *Vixen*.

"What men are you?" asked the tall man with a field man's bluntness.

"We are the crew and wardens," said Sergeant Evenage, "of Her Majesty's Ship the *Swan*. Caulkers have left a leak along her keel, and we are making good the defect."

"The *Swan*, out of Portsmouth," inquired the tall farmer, "as is captained by Captain Hawkins?"

"That very ship, my good man," said Evenage, with a smile that betrayed a trace of doubt.

The tall man took a better grip on the shaft of his bill-hook. The dogs growled in unison, although they remained on their haunches near the younger man. Sherwin thought that he had never seen such intimidating beasts, nor any so eager to tear intruders to shreds.

"And you prick pigs, do you, for pitch?" asked the tall farmer.

"We hear such praise of the livestock in this region," replied Evenage, "that our shipmate could not restrain his curiosity regarding the quality and general merits of your piggery."

"There is a sailing *Swan*," said the farmer, speaking in the slightly impatient accent of a man who saved such arguments for market day. "But as to whether Hawkins captains her, or whether she berths in Plymouth, I have no knowledge."

Evenage let his shoulders rise and fall, and he lifted a gloved hand in helpless courtesy.

"We intend no harm," interjected Sherwin, "to any living creature."

But Tryce's quivering animosity gave the lie to the cordial fictions of Sherwin and the sergeant.

"Percy," said the landsman, in a voice empty of all fear, "hurry up to Fairleigh and tell Sir Anthony that his land is despoiled not by Spaniards, as we feared, but by English pirates."

16

W E ARE NOT PIRATES," said Evenage.
He made this protest in the affable, round tones of a lawyer addressing a magistrate.

The farmer made no remark in response.

"If you will send word to your lord," added Evenage, "be kind enough to give him the compliments and best wishes of Captain Brandon Fletcher, the strong right hand of our gracious Queen."

"Did you get that?" the farmer asked the youthful Percy, who turned back to catch these additional words. "Tell Sir Anthony that the famous Captain Fletcher is on our doorstep."

The younger man hurried off.

"Although," the farmer added, quietly, "I hear that in a crowd of honest men, Captain Fletcher would be missing."

Evenage gave his sword belt a hitch, and Sherwin sensed that this veiled insult might be answered with blood.

"I give my word, before God," said Sherwin, eager to intervene, "that no harm will come to man or beast."

Evenage took a moment to adjust his hat, as though in surprise or instant caution at hearing Sherwin utter such an unenforceable oath.

The farmer lifted his chin in recognition of the veteran soldier's reluctance. "Can the same be said for all of you," asked the farmer, "or will my dogs have seamen for dinner?"

"We'll do no harm, my good man," said Evenage, assuming a lighthearted tone, "upon my word."

Tryce spat. "I'll not bandy oaths with a swineherd."

Evenage turned and cuffed him. The blow was hard enough to snap Tryce's teeth together and send him staggering back across the rutted road.

The farmer took a step back, and Sherwin, too, had shied involuntarily at this sudden violence. This was not the first time that Sherwin was forcibly aware that his assumptions and hopes might not fit the actual character of his new companions.

"The young gentleman and I," said Evenage, "will take responsibility for this sailor."

Tryce leaned against the wall, setting his cap back snugly onto his head. He made a point of spitting deliberately in the direction of the landsman, and Sherwin did not like the way Sergeant Evenage wrapped his hand around the hilt of his sword, drawing the blade and settling it back into its scabbard.

"Tell me, pray, whose farmland is this?" asked Sherwin,

as much to guide the silence toward friendly discourse as to solicit an answer.

The farmer, however, did not like the way Tryce was scowling, leaning against the wall, and gazing at the sergeant. The farmer retreated into a guarded silence, giving his head a shake in response to Sherwin's inquiry, much the way a solitary traveler might refuse to speak to a suddenly menacing group of beggars.

The four of them were kept where they were, watched over by the dogs, which grew bored with threatening the strangers and began to yawn and sniff the ground nearby.

Sherwin and his companion could observe young Percy's progress toward a large house in the distance.

Whatever meeting transpired there did not take long.

As they watched, they beheld the opening under the gatehouse swing wide and the mantled form that had been visible on the cliffside reappeared. She was joined by a male figure who looked, at a distance, to be a serving-man, clad in a gray cloak and wearing a broadsword.

No stylish individual carried such a weapon, which was thought to be manly, essentially English, but entirely unfashionable. Nonetheless, Sherwin did not enjoy the prospect of being cut by one.

As the woman approached, Sherwin became aware that the striking, soldierly appearance of his garments was diminished by the spattering of muck and worse over his boots. He was aware, too, how even a short voyage with merchant seamen had made the prospect of quiet, pleasant conversation with a young woman seem extraordinary and desirable.

The sergeant also removed his cap, gave it a quick brush-off with a gloved hand, and then it was too late to repair the outward show they made as the young woman swept quickly toward them, the servant with a firm grip on the pommel of his sword.

Sherwin readied any number of dashing opening comments—compliments on the weather, sincere respects regarding the attractiveness of the fields and oaks all around—but it was Tryce who got off the first remark, a whisper, but one that carried.

"We'll stick and pickle this lady," he said, "if we can't capture a pig."

The sergeant gave a twitch of embarrassment and Sherwin took a step sideways, trying to distance himself from the sullen seaman. There was, at least, the hope that the young woman had not been able to hear the remark.

The young woman introduced herself, sweeping back the hood of her mantle with one gloved hand, and asked, "Which of you is Captain Fletcher?"

17

KATHARINE WESTING had light brown hair and brown eyes, and was not afraid to look at each man directly, including Tryce, who made a great show of finally realizing that a lady was present and removing his cap. Bartholomew made a courteous and graceful bow.

"None of us, my lady," said Sergeant Evenage, "is equal to the honor of that name."

"My father would meet with the captain over wine and nourishing fare," said Katharine. "He has a proposition that may put money into the captain's purse." She added, "That man is bleeding."

Tryce shook his head in denial. "I never," he said.

"Oh, don't mind our Tryce, my lady," said Sergeant Evenage. "He bleeds or he doesn't, as the wind blows."

"If your people, my lady," said Sherwin, "could offer some dressing for our companion's wound, we would be grateful."

This was the first remark he had made in Katharine's presence, and she smiled to hear the words, as though reassured that she was encountering human beings of normal fellow-feeling.

Sherwin introduced himself, giving his Christian name and his surname, and his place of birth. As he spoke, he felt the need to be far from Tryce and even the well-spoken sergeant. Instead, he wanted to be strolling in a sun-drenched garden where he could weave verses for this young lady. He had never felt this way so strongly, and the feeling struck Sherwin with all the fierceness of a too-long-suppressed insight. What he did not want, at that moment, was a further voyage, and the company of bungling rogues like Tryce.

"Oh, this is our new young gentleman and historian, my lady," interjected Sergeant Evenage, as though eager to provide additional introduction. "As was nearly killed by the sea this recent night."

Sherwin was pleased at this description of his character and recent adventures, and he was sure that he must have blushed before he could speak. He sensed Bartholomew standing tall beside him, proud of his new master.

This good feeling was offset as Lady Katharine asked, "Tell me, Sherwin Morris—are you a brigand, too?"

Sherwin was about to express himself handsomely when a goose, whose trumpeted complaints had carried from an unseen confinement until now, made its appearance.

The large white bird careened around the corner of the wall and lunged at everything in sight, including the larger of the dogs, the sergeant's boot tops, and as much as it could pinch in its yellow beak of Bartholomew's breeches.

The goose's great mistake, however, was in attacking Tryce.

The seaman did not tolerate being assaulted for an instant.

He drew his sword from its scabbard, took a single cut through the air, and the goose was headless, even as its unfurled wings and churning legs continued to hurry the remains out across the road.

The decapitated white fowl was blushing into a rosy hue as its blood cascaded down over its plumage, and still the bird ran, continuing in an uneven circuit. Sherwin felt called upon to end an episode of grotesque cruelty, and to assert something like his own stamp on events.

He drew the pistol from his belt, sparing a glance toward Bartholomew, who gave the hint of miming a two-handed grip.

Sherwin cocked, aimed, and fired.

THE REPORT was deafening. The smoke was a bright blue in the sunlight, and smelled strongly of sulfur.

Even with a horizon obscured by smoke, Sherwin could see that his shot went wide of the headless bird, and that his attempt to cancel the post-mortem sprint with a further act was doomed. The shot had sent up a spray of soil, and then Sherwin could see the lead ball as it bounded, slightly deformed from the impact with the dirt, like a hazelnut tossed across the grass.

But the goose's body took that moment to collapse and utterly expire, as though the sound of the pistol shot had torn some fabric in what remained of its will. The thought was not pure fancy. People believed that cannon shots often caused rain, and during a drought farmers sometimes loaded their fowling pieces and set out across the fields to puncture the blue with gunfire.

When Sherwin was able to hear at all, he made out the words of Katharine as she said, "Well done, Sherwin Morris."

Sherwin turned to Bartholomew and said, with words sounding strange in his still-ringing ears, "Get coin from Tryce to pay for this."

Tryce wrestled free of Bartholomew, but not before a leather sack was winkled from the interior of his tunic, and silver pennies taken, enough to pay for a burgeoning flock of prize geese. As Sherwin had suspected, a mountebank's apprentice learned the fine points of theft.

Sherwin pressed the silver into the farmer's hand and then he turned to address Katharine.

"My lady," he said, "I am sorry you had to see this."

Sherwin had known many women before, including an intimate entanglement with Lily Sprocket, the daughter of the owner of the Cock and Miter inn. He had thought himself in love with Lily, and ruefully advised himself to forever keep a closer guard on his affections when Lily took up with an ostler from Epping, found herself pregnant, and married him.

Sherwin had never met a woman like Katharine Westing. She had a direct, lively gaze and a ready smile. But she also had that indefinable quality so often described as beauty.

"My dear Sherwin," said Katharine with a smile, "I have seen many things worse."

"My lady," said Sherwin—feeling his earnest intentions never to love again slipping away—"I regret to hear it."

He took the offered gloved hand, the white leather of the glove well cured and not a mean piece of stitchery, either. But for all the expense of the silk lining of her mantle, lavender showing well against the heath-brown of the hood, there was a tear in her sleeve that had been daintily mended, and a fray along the instep of her shoe. She was well appointed, but not as wealthy as she had been in the recent past.

"I suppose," she said, "a felon such as yourself fires a pistol before breakfast every day."

"My lady," was all he could think of saying, "if it pleases you."

BUT TRYCE did not leave at once.

"I'll not retreat to the ship," he told Sherwin, "without the captain's pig, as he requested, and payment from your lad for the money he took." His leg was still bleeding, and no one had given another thought to his medical needs.

Katharine had gone back toward the great house in the distance, taking her sword-wearing servant with her, and Evenage was trying to lead Tryce away with a soothing *Now, now,* like a dockside constable calming an angry drunk.

"Mr. Highbridge," the sergeant said, "will find a way to pay you back for your trouble."

"I want payment now," said Tryce.

"As for compensation," Sherwin could not restrain himself from saying, "you owe us all for saving your life, covering your disgrace, and not delivering you over to those hungry dogs."

Tryce gave a shake of his shoulders, and Evenage released him.

"Do I?" said Tryce, smoothing down his sleeves with a show of dignity. "Shall we simply forget all about this, then?"

"As you wish," said Sherwin shortly.

"Until, as it happens," added Tryce, "I beat the coin out of your little lifter, when his new master is playing cock pigeon with his white-gloved doxy."

A lifter was a street thief, on a level with pickpockets and fruit-stall filchers, and Sherwin took offense at this slur against Bartholomew. As for the insult against his respect for Lady Katharine, and for the lady's good name, Sherwin had seen gentlemen on Fleet Street draw their blades and use them for less.

But he made no quick remark, and he kept his sword in its sheath, with an effort of will.

There would be plenty of opportunity in the future to teach Tryce good manners—perhaps even at the point of a sword.

V

BLOOD ON HIS
DOUBLET

18

"ALL RIGHT, FATHER, it's done," Katharine said. "I did as you requested—I have sent for Captain Fletcher. The seamen will return to visit us at day's end."

Sir Anthony had rolled out one of his rare sea charts, this one printed in Holland, showing the Atlantic with the Azores puckering the sea's white expanse like wounds that had imperfectly healed.

"Now, Father," she said, sitting down before the fire and tugging off her gloves, "tell me what you are planning."

She held the empty leather fingers up to her lips. She imagined the touch of Sherwin's hand, the way his warm grasp would feel unprotected by leather. She had encountered many men in her role as hostess of Fairleigh. They had been shipwrights and navigators, shipping agents and knights. But no one had caught her eye like the young man with sunny brown hair and traces of blood on his doublet.

She wanted to see him again, and in fact spend more

than a small amount of time with him. She wanted this very much, and she was willing to run some risk to bring this opportunity about.

If only she could think of a way.

"Planning?" Sir Anthony was asking with a sideways smile. "What possible mischief can I be up to, inviting a notorious sea rake in for some roast capon?"

"And baked goose, too," said Katharine.

"Heaven has sent us a goose?" asked Anthony.

A visiting goose sometimes descended from the sky, or wandered in from some far-off place, like an itinerant scold. For all their bad temper, geese were social animals and drawn to flocks of other geese, ducks, chickens; and one goose to Katharine's certain knowledge had taken up protective residence with a brood of rabbits.

"Maggie," she said, "fell into the hands of a particularly unpleasant sailor."

She briefly recounted the cruel incident that had befallen the goose well known enough to have earned an affectionate nickname.

"Poor Maggie," said Anthony wistfully. "The Spaniards for all their steel would not have had a chance with her to protect us."

Katharine wished her friends could meet Sherwin and his seagoing companions. She had paid a visit to her old friend Eleanor that morning, to see how her windmill survived the blustery night. Eleanor and her husband were happy. Their joy was easy to perceive, as easy as

watching the sunlight fall from the sky. Clement Wood-
field, Eleanor's husband, had a rugged, horselike quality,
and a horse's contentment in work. Whenever Katharine
saw him, he was lifting a sack of grain, or plying a rake,
or using an awl to mend a harness. His family had thrived
as potters, joiners, and millers as long as anyone could
recall.

Clement had a survivor's instinct for avoiding trouble,
and he had heard that a great Spanish fleet was expected
to raid the south of England and leave not a moorhen
alive. He had been sharpening his wood ax into a weapon,
and grinding a billhook into a battle-pike. He was considering sending Eleanor to Winchester, to get her away
from the coast.

"You can guess," Anthony was saying, "what my strategy
is, can't you?"

He was not well today—his ulcerated leg was hurting.
But on days when he was most beset by pain, his spirits
were the keenest. He stirred the fire now, and then limped
around the hall, thrusting the fire iron into shadows like a
rapier.

She said, "Please tell me."

"Guess."

"I will not make a sport of this, Father."

He smiled, and stabbed the iron into the fire, ringing it
against the firedogs supporting the blazing log. "Katharine, we will steal our own vessel."

She had suspected this, without allowing herself to seriously entertain the prospect. She felt both excitement at the plausibility of the scheme, and dismay at the risk.

"I don't think that I am equal to actually sailing the high seas myself," he continued, "and so we'll pay Fletcher to do it for us. And he will, I have no doubt."

The idea thrilled her. The proposal had the merits of surprise as well as adventure, and it was a ruse that grasping Pevensey, for all his brisk and tireless avarice, would not have anticipated.

"Where will you put our stolen *Rosebriar*," she asked, "so Pevensey and his agents will not find her?"

"Near Saint Mawes, on an inlet along the Cornish coast," he said, indicating another map rolled up on the side table. "We'll hide her from Pevensey, and after a few weeks I'll ease the ship up to Bristol, sit down with my negotiators there, and make inquiries as to selling a few tons of fine cinnamon."

"It might succeed," she conceded. She was beginning to entertain the bare beginning of another possibility.

"My scheme is sure to work," argued Anthony. "I can see no defect in the proposal at all."

"Unless Pevensey hears of it," she said, "or discovers the truth afterward."

"By then it won't matter," said Anthony. "We'll have our money."

She did not speak again for a long moment, lost in thought. "I am hopeful," she said at length, "but I am also uneasy."

"About Fletcher? At heart, I warrant that he's a man much like me."

"No," she said. "I'm not worried about the famous captain. I am concerned about the men with him."

"What sort of sailors are they?" he asked.

She could not respond for the moment. Her father was a clever man, and practical. He was a dreamer who nonetheless knew how to act in the world of real folk and rugged events. But he was not experienced with every breed of human nature.

There were individuals worse even than Pevensey and his hirelings, and some of them might sail on the *Vixen.* The character of such rough folk did much to make her question the wisdom of her own embryonic plan.

"Father, what do you know of Captain Fletcher?"

"I knew the man to exchange greetings with back on Leadenhall Street," Anthony was saying, "when I built craft for the Admiralty. So when I hear that the captain of the pirates teeming over our land is no nameless killer but England's remarkable sea dog, I begin to let my mind fly with the swifts."

"How does the approach of war," asked Katharine, "make your plan all the more crucial?"

"Because we need to get the *Rosebriar* into a hiding place where the Spaniards can't sack her."

"And me, too," suggested Katharine.

"Yes," her father admitted, "I wish I could think of a safe place to secure you, as well." It was like him to plunge from sharp enthusiasm to cloudy concern in an instant. She put her hand over his.

"Fortiter in re," she said, quoting part of one of her father's favorite axioms.

Mighty in deed.

He gave an appreciative chuckle, but the concern lingered in his eyes.

KATHARINE WAS SURE of it now—she had a plan of her own.

19

B UT HOW WAS IT, Bartholomew," asked Sherwin,
"that you could hide a scorpion under your tongue?"

The two were hurrying along the road back toward the
ship, behind Tryce and the sergeant. Evenage kept one
arm around Tryce, but the injured seaman's head could be
seen jerking and swiveling as the man's ill humor continued undiminished, and he voiced complaints without
cease.

Sherwin thought that it might prove prudent to walk
faster and reach the *Vixen* and the captain well in advance
of Tryce. But hurrying ahead seemed inappropriate, and
even a little undignified, so Sherwin stayed a short stone's
throw behind the sergeant and the fuming seaman.

"As to the scorpion," said Bartholomew, "the little mon-
ster's stinger, sir, was cut off."

"But nevertheless, dear Bartholomew—what a disagree-
able duty you had to perform."

"My shipboard life is easier." Bartholomew sighed. "But

my mountebank master loved to sing, and he was fond of ladies and cats."

"Do you miss him?"

"My master is in prison for failing to cure an illness," said Bartholomew by way of answer, a little sadly, it seemed to Sherwin.

"What sort of illness?" Sherwin inquired.

"A gentleman in Calais, a captain's clerk, had not voided his bladder, sir, for many days," said Bartholomew. "He was in pain."

"It sorrows me to hear it," said Sherwin.

"My master sometimes performed the necessary operation, a quick in-and-out with a long blade or bodkin, and then always slipped from town the same day, sir, because all such operations end the same way."

"What way is that?"

"Sir, the operation relieves the crisis, but then the patient dies."

Bartholomew walked in silence for a few strides, and then he said, "My master stayed in Calais because he loved a lady, sir."

"Did he?" asked Sherwin, not paying Bartholomew's account full attention just then.

He was trying to think of ways to see Lady Katharine again, and he was deeply troubled that, unless the captain sought his companionship this evening, he might never have the opportunity.

Sherwin and the boy descended the cliff path, and it

was clear at once to Sherwin that he should have taken pains to reach the vessel before Tryce.

The ship's carpenter was placing his tools into a leather holder and rolling the leather up into a bundle. Men with mauls hammered away at the barnacles that were unseen from Sherwin's angle as he drew near the vessel. The seamen were folding their clothing, and setting out the most stubbornly moist mantles and cloaks on rocks near the cliff. The ship's company had the air of a group that had been steadily at work, and whose chores were gradually being completed.

The captain and Highbridge were consulting on the waterline, and from time to time the men looked up from their conversation to glance at the lookout on the cliff.

The boatswain Lockwood was listening with an air of reluctant skepticism to Tryce as the man held forth, and even though the sergeant stood nearby and shook his head, negating what was being said, Tryce's loud complaints were gathering a small congregation.

"And then the lad Bartholomew took a knife he keeps in secret," Tryce was saying, "and he slit me in the leg, here." The blood, which had ceased to flow, was beginning to ooze again, as though to authenticate Tryce's fictitious report.

The seamen stirred, murmuring unhappily.

"And then the little weasel was in my purse," Tryce went on, "and taking as much silver as his nasty little fist could grab."

"That's not as it happened," the sergeant said. But even as he spoke Sherwin could tell by a few scattered chuckles that, although Tryce was considered to be the source of dramatic retellings, this most recent account was not necessarily considered to be fact. Sherwin surmised also that the sergeant, although respected, was not always believed, either. His protest was met with no great interest.

The surgeon, however, was not laughing.

The physician made his way over to where Tryce was standing, ignoring the seaman's report of a pig the size of a fishing boat. Dr. Reynard knelt, examining the wound on Tryce's leg with a critical eye, and when the doctor stood he said something quiet into the dour seaman's ear.

"You will not ever," protested the seaman.

"If that limb stays joined to your body, my man," said the surgeon, "it will fester."

"And so fester yourself," responded Tryce.

"If the leg rots," said the doctor, "so you will, too."

"And thus," said Tryce, raising his voice and indicating Bartholomew with a theatrical gesture, "it is not enough that this lad Bartholomew winkles me out of ducats, but he tries to steal my leg as well."

20

SHERWIN CAUGHT the gleam of spitefulness in Tryce's eye.

Tryce had decided that his power to defame and slur a gentleman like Sherwin, who was apparently in favor with Highbridge and the captain, was not very great. But Bartholomew was not so well regarded, and was open to slander.

Furthermore, attacking Bartholomew was a sly and effective way to harm Sherwin, and Tryce's manner seemed to indicate that in his present poisonous humor he would lose both legs, both arms, and perhaps even his head, if it would harm the newly arrived gentleman.

Bartholomew folded his arms.

"I'll explain what happened, Bartholomew," confided Sherwin quietly but, he hoped, reassuringly.

"Say what you will, sir," said Bartholomew, "when folk decide against you, your name is worthless."

Sherwin stepped to Tryce's side and put his arm around the seaman, who kept his body at a stubborn position.

"Tryce was bravely set on finding a grand pig for our table," said Sherwin, with a heartiness that was nearly entirely assumed. "Just as Captain Fletcher desired. And he found such a worthy quarry, too. But this beast proved to have the disposition of a fiend—nine devils, filled with fury, each individual sprite in this sow's soul bent on rending our friend Tryce here open like a fish."

Tryce softened his posture and his frame gave a slight shiver at the recollection. He sighed. "She was a huge, vicious pig," he said, "and I doubt we should let her go unpunished."

"For what?" asked Sherwin, giving Tryce a meaningful pat on the back.

Tryce looked down at the pebble-strewn beach, and Sherwin realized that the seaman, for all his obstinate rancor, was a man facing the consequences of an injury. No thinking man wanted to spend what might prove to be his last few days as a mortal bearing false witness.

"For the attacking of my leg," said Tryce.

The assembled men relaxed into a good-natured throng, expressing regret at Tryce's injury and adding congratulations to Sherwin.

At that moment the lookout high on the cliff sang, "*Sail-ho!*"

The cry was almost happy, the sentinel's voice being lit by the thrill of having spied a vessel after a long, uneventful vigil.

But then the lookout added, "Nine sails—ten—southwest by west," and his call was unmistakably anxious.

THE CREW fell silent.

Sherwin had the sickening, fearful thought that the Spanish fleet had made its appearance.

A row of sails, a dozen at least, glided along the horizon, heading east toward Southampton and Portsmouth, the great seaports and unprotected farmland of England.

The sails were full, and the dark shapes of the hulls barely visible. At this great distance, even on the clear afternoon, movement was impossible to discern, only the presence of stubborn apparitions that had not been there a little while ago, and now represented a tidy multitude, intent on the wind.

Captain Fletcher walked among his men, giving them comfort.

"It's only Drake," he said. "With his scouting fleet, heading back toward Portsmouth. He's been looking for the Armada off Ushant, beyond the far reaches of Brittany, and by all appearances he hasn't had any luck."

FLETCHER JOINED SHERWIN and Sergeant Evenage at the high-tide mark, where a line of driftwood showed where the tide would reach as the hour approached midnight.

"Why, yes," the captain said, "it sounds like a delightful evening prospect. I do recall Anthony Westing well," he added. "We rescued a mastiff pup from the Thames, one of the losers from a South Bank pit fight. His owner evidently threw the animal into the river in a fit of unhappiness or penury, and we kept it from drowning."

"Why couldn't Drake find the Spanish fleet?" Sherwin asked.

"Drake does well," said Fletcher, "to find his left boot next to his right."

"Is it," Sherwin persisted, "because the sea is such an immense place to hide?"

Highbridge had joined them, and he listened intently to his captain's response.

"The sea is round in all directions," said Fletcher, "and boundless, as well. But for a fighting sea force, with appalling intentions, there are not many logical places from which to stage an attack."

"If the Armada was not off the coast of France," queried Sherwin, "where could it be?"

"Perhaps," said Fletcher with just a hint of impatience at such ceaseless questions, "the King of Spain has no such navy."

"But, Captain, you don't believe that, do you?" asked Highbridge.

The first officer had not broken his silence before this, and his question had a searching bluntness that was close to insubordinate.

"Do I not?" queried Fletcher with a disingenuous smile.

"No, sir," said Highbridge, in a voice that was calm but

insistent. "And, if you'll permit me to say so, you don't intend to stay out of the fight, either."

"There," said Fletcher, "good Highbridge, I fear I shall thwart you."

FLETCHER WALKED ALONE down to the waterline, the low tide banking and backing, the foam streaming sluggishly down to the surf.

"He knows where the Spanish are," confided Highbridge to Sherwin. "Drake can't find the Spaniards, but our captain can."

"Why doesn't he help discover them?" asked Sherwin.

Highbridge had no answer.

Fletcher gazed out across the sun-splashed water of the Channel.

The sails of Drake's scouting fleet, which seemed not to move, were nonetheless well to the east of where they had been first sighted, and closer, too, each vessel heeling with the southwest wind.

The Spanish warships were, by all accounts, considerably larger, and bristled with heavier artillery than any English ship, culverins and demiculverins of great weight and caliber. Sherwin tried to imagine what an armada of one hundred ships, or more, would be like.

The consideration filled him with alarm. But with a certain thrill, too, as he tried to envision such power.

21

THE HEARTH FIRE was bright, gently illuminating Fairleigh's great hall, the light reaching all the way to the griffin tapestry on the wall.

"Sherwin is going to write a history of my life, if not up to and including my death," said Captain Fletcher. "Sherwin is the author of *The King of Spain Bearded in His Den and His Staunchest Ships Reduced to Kindling.*"

"I read that," said Sir Anthony. "I have it here on my shelf—I found the pamphlet magnificent. I recall your description of the cannon fire Captain Drake encountered: 'Ragged bursts made instant morning of the night, and black tide blazed in echoed flames.' "

"Such narration is a wonder!" exclaimed Katharine.

To his surprise, the feelings uppermost in Sherwin's heart included self-conscious embarrassment. He was pleased that Sir Anthony and Katharine acknowledged his skill, but he was also keenly aware that he knew but little of actual warfare. The prose of his well-received pamphlet suddenly seemed forced to Sherwin, and he wished that it was not too late to alter the description.

"You do me, Sir Anthony," said Sherwin, "too great an honor."

Captain Fletcher sipped a cup of the brandywine he had brought himself, a gift for his host and his daughter. He said crisply, "I believe our young scholar's talents can be directed to more worthy subjects."

Sherwin caught Katharine's eye from time to time, and she began to think that perhaps she had been too forward with this newcomer.

She had offered Sherwin her hand with Maggie the goose lying there headless and trembling, and it seemed to her now that she had made every show of familiarity short of an actual embrace. She felt a little embarrassed at her behavior, and so she made up her mind that she would not meet his eyes, not once, all through dinner.

Katharine observed the captain closely. So much depended on his character, and during the meal she listened to his quiet laugh, and enjoyed the memories he shared with her father, cockfights and boat races along the Thames during their younger years.

She wanted to be able to trust him, for her own sake as well as her father's, but she had lingering misgivings.

"This brandywine you have given us, Captain Fletcher," said Anthony, "is excellent."

"Stolen, my friend," said Fletcher. "Everything I own is the fruit of crime."

"Where did you pilfer these fine wine spirits?" asked Katharine, increasingly captivated by the captain's unusual combination of winning frankness and self-confessed roguery.

"We sailed up the river Lima in a pinnace," Captain Fletcher recalled, "during a three-quarter moon. We helped ourselves to more spirits than we could carry—we had to abandon a few casks on the Ponte de Lima. Portuguese brandy has a moody, tarry character, and it pleases me."

The captain had sent word that he would be pleased to visit Fairleigh Hall, and every effort had been made to prepare a welcome feast. Chickens had been gutted and plucked, and honey and cloves had been stirred into the indifferent wine, hoping to swell it into something appetizing. And there was the goose, stuffed with what was left of last autumn's apples.

The food had been delicious, disguising well Fairleigh's frugal prospects. The dishes and servingware were fired clay and pewter, marked with the insignia of Fairleigh, a griffin *regardant*.

Katharine had always been fond of this symbol, although the griffin was a beast that elicited her pity with its ardent attempt at fierceness. He was half eagle and half lion, but that did not account for the creature's expression, turning back to scold a pursuer. She was not convinced that the Fairleigh griffin was anything to be afraid of. The creature no one could love looked back hopefully, it seemed to her, and not fiercely at all. Katharine could love it, in truth, and everything else about Fairleigh.

The group was small—Sir Anthony and his daughter, Captain Fletcher and Sherwin Morris, along with the dark-clad Highbridge with his quiet smile. The hour was early evening, with the sunny summer day taking a long time to give way to night. Bartholomew and Evenage dined at a side table, observant but silent.

Baines was dressed in his best smock and wore his finest cocked hat as he waited on the table. He had gone over to Dunham that afternoon and traded as much cheese as he could convey in a wheelbarrow for two choice laying hens.

"Are you an enemy of the Portuguese?" asked Katharine. Portugal, as Katharine knew, was a sometime ally and trading partner of England, and often suffered at the hands of the militant Spanish.

"I would never say that I am any man's foe, in particular," said Captain Fletcher.

"How can it be you are such a relentless thief," asked Katharine, "being, as you seem, a man of merit?"

"You pay me a compliment, Lady Katharine."

She was impressed by the captain's appearance, and the way his offhand, easy manner barely disguised a cutting intensity. She could easily imagine a young woman being won over by his attentions.

"But I do not seek to flatter you, Captain," she responded after a pause. "I want to know."

"Take our well-known hero Drake as an example," said

the captain. "He voyaged around the globe with over five score men in his crew, returned to Greenwich with scant two dozen remaining, and those living skeletons kept together by lice and scurvy scabs. I have seen brave men with their bellies shot out, and I have seen soldiers run through heart and lung, guttering for breath. I steal because I am crafty enough to avoid killing, and because I hate to see my men bleed."

"But this does not answer the question, Captain, if you please," Katharine persisted. "Why you do not ply a trade as a master of law or a scholar of the sea, or any other honorable profession?"

"Katharine," protested Sir Anthony, "you press our guest too hard."

But Sherwin leaned forward, very interested, she thought, in Fletcher's possible response.

"I am as honest with myself as I wish other men were," said Fletcher with a laugh. "As a young clerk, through dint of hard work and talent, I rose up to the station of controller of the Queen's Navy, if I may make a painful and lengthy story brief. I made sure that every purser was prudent, and that every strake and sheet were accounted for. I was good at what I did, but I was envied."

Katharine liked the captain's manner. He had a way of looking at his audience, winning their attention, and then letting his gaze wander, firelight in his eyes.

"Why," she asked, "were you envied?"

"Men wished they could occupy my position, Lady

Katharine," the captain continued, "so that they could profit. They accused me of being a dishonest man, and while I was no thief, I was a man touched with the sin of pride. I resigned in a foul temper, and decided that if people thought me a thief, why, then, that's what I would be."

"Surely, Captain," said Katharine, with what she hoped was not ill-mannered directness, "you had a choice."

The captain lifted a hand from the table and quietly let it fall, as though to say such further examination of his own nature did not interest him.

He reflected for a moment, however. "I was raised in Dover," he explained. "My father was a purchaser for the Royal Navy, and I was well accustomed to tides and the compass rose, being a sailor since my youth. After my dishonor, I took to the sea. I suffered a thief's reputation, and I decided that I would enjoy a robber's swag. And so I do, and I regret nothing."

"You might well say, sir, that you are a trustworthy man in a disguise," said Sherwin hopefully.

Perhaps, thought Katharine, he wanted to preserve a positive outlook on the moral fiber of the captain he served.

"No," said the captain emphatically, drawing the word out and then laughing. "No, I was always going to be as you see me."

"But you are careful with the health of your shipmates," suggested Sherwin.

"Ah, and there you have me cornered, my wise young

historian. Not a fortnight ago, I tried to steal a prize ship from some of Drake's colleagues, and lost four of my soldiers in the fighting. I was badly upset by this failure on my part to protect their lives. This is why I am so reluctant to see my ship take part in any glorious battle to safeguard our kingdom. I detest bloodshed, and I am too softhearted, I think, to serve as a sword-wielding warrior."

"But if Drake and Frobisher win further glory in a great battle," asked Sherwin, "and perhaps take prizes, won't you envy them?"

"Envy is a sin, good Sherwin," said the captain, "as I am sure you know."

"And are you not a sinner?" asked Katharine.

"Oh, more than many, and less than some," said the captain with a quiet laugh. "But come now—why did you ask me here? What is this scheme our noble baronet promised would further lard my strongbox?"

"Katharine knows the particulars," said Sir Anthony. "Explain to our guests, if you will, Katharine, the details of our deception."

SHE HAD NOT EXPECTED her father to ask her to disclose their intentions.

She was surprised, but she was also pleased at his trust in her. Just as so much of Fairleigh's future relied on the captain's character, so much depended on her now.

22

KATHARINE HAD ALWAYS LOVED the way firelight and its diminutive cousin, candlelight, made the world look.

With the slow summer dusk coming on, the faces around her now were gilded and silent, intent only on her. Katharine was especially fascinated by the way Sherwin leaned forward, his eyes bright with encouragement.

Their predicament was easily described, and Sherwin's eyes grew brighter as he heard the details of the *Rosebriar* and the ship's likely route from the Azores.

"Her captain was born and bred in Cornwall, and he always hugs the coast there as he returns," she continued. She took pains to delineate the character of Pevensey, and his representative, Sir Gregory. "We are offering you one-third of the value of the cargo to help us."

"Sir Gregory," said Sherwin, when her account was concluded, "should be beaten, my lady, and any of his men with him. And as for Pevensey—" Strong feeling made it impossible to conclude his thoughts.

"There is not a man here," said Captain Fletcher, in a tone of sympathy, "who would not see the grasping nobleman whipped."

"Indeed," said Sherwin, "and worse than that."

"Beating his lordship to a pudding," said the captain, "will not fatten your purse, Sherwin, but a few plump prizes will."

"Captain, if you please," said Sherwin, "is there no aspiration more important than silver?"

"None at all," said the captain. "But what makes you and your father think that, having taken the ship, Lady Katharine, I will share the prize with her rightful owner?"

"And what makes you think that, once you have stolen her," replied Katharine, "my father and I might not report you to the Admiralty, and squeeze a reward from them?"

The captain gave a sly smile. "I would tell the Admiralty of your scheme."

"They would not take your word," Sir Anthony interjected, "over the oath of a baronet who has never stolen so much as a farthing in his life." He kept his tone friendly, but with a decided edge.

"I know of a way," said Katharine, "to ensure that the captain behaves honorably, and to make sure that Captain Loy of the *Rosebriar* understands our plan. After all," she added, "we would not want Captain Loy to sink our Captain Fletcher's ship in earnest error."

Her father straightened in his chair. "Katharine, I begin

to believe I anticipate your plan," he said, "and I don't like it."

"I shall go on board the *Vixen* myself," said Katharine, "to see that Captain Fletcher lives up to his part of the bargain."

"This is the worst plan I have ever heard," said Sir Anthony.

The captain smiled. "No, she may have me pinned, your wise daughter. Because with her as a witness I will have to either turn complete scoundrel, and deliver her to the Devil, or live up to my word and help you to steal your own ship."

Sir Anthony protested again. "I cannot abide such an arrangement."

"And I shall be far away from the coast, Father," said Katharine, "safe from any attack the Spaniards might loose on these estates."

"Safe where?" said Anthony. "On the high seas with this distinguished rascal?"

"He is the man you trust with your future," said Katharine. "Besides, my voyage will last only as long as it takes to intercept our cargo."

"Katharine," said Anthony ruefully, "you argue too well."

"There is another reason," said the captain, "that makes your idea, Lady Katharine, appealing from my standpoint."

"What is that, Captain?" asked Highbridge.

Highbridge had not spoken during most of the meal,

and, after introductions had been made, he had taken in what was said and, Katharine thought, noticed what was pointedly not mentioned.

He was a lean man, garbed in black or the darkest possible blue. His beard was combed to a point, and he carried a lens of crystal on a golden chain around his neck. Just as Fletcher radiated an air of impish contradiction, Highbridge gave the impression of quiet single-mindedness.

"With this lady on board, Highbridge," said Fletcher, "there is no question that we can take part in any fighting. We must stay out of the war—if in truth the war comes."

"I am relieved to hear it," sighed Sir Anthony.

"You'll not use my presence on board the *Vixen*," protested Katharine, "to excuse yourself from fighting for our Queen."

"My lady, I am reassured," said Highbridge.

She would dread to take part in a battle, and would be quite pleased if any forthcoming war was forestalled indefinitely. But she bridled at the implication that she was a frail nestling, in need of protection. Furthermore, she could guess how a mariner like Highbridge might resent her presence on his ship, if it kept the *Vixen* out of her chance at glory.

"And the presence of a lovely lady, if you will permit me," said the captain, with a gallant gesture in Katharine's direction, "might empower my historian to describe the *Vixen* and her captain in lines of poetry."

"I have begun," said Sherwin, with an air of hopeful modesty, "knitting such verses."

"Let us hear a sample," insisted the captain.

"They are fledgling lines only," said Sherwin, "and not ready for flight."

"We desire to listen to them," said Captain Fletcher.

Sherwin touched a cup of sweetened wine to his lips and said, in his clear, pleasing voice,

> *"Our pikes like hedgepig quills, and our bright sails*
> *Like morning's sunlight seconded from dawn,*
> *If Heaven is content to lend us triumph,*
> *In what torn vessel should we fear?"*

This brief fragment of poetry—which to Katharine sounded very fine indeed—was met by a silence of anticipation.

Sherwin ducked his head. He felt profoundly stirred by everything Katharine had said, and keenly resentful toward Lord Pevensey and Sir Gregory.

"That's all I have finished just now," he said.

"A sterling fragment, dear Sherwin, but a shard only," said the captain with a happy laugh. "Think what glorious verse you'll be inspired to compose with this noble young lady aboard our vessel."

Sherwin had the good grace, Katharine noted, to blush.

But any further conversation was interrupted by the distant sound of an approaching horse, adorned with bells, judging by the sound. Additional hooves clattered in the dooryard, and Baines hurried into the room.

"Sir Gregory is here, my lords, with Cecil Rawes," said the servant, "demanding to see Sir Anthony."

Anthony looked alarmed. "You must hide, Fletcher, all of you."

Captain Fletcher rose, and so did Highbridge and Sherwin, but they made no effort to leave the room. They did, however, fasten on their rapiers as Baines handed the weapons around to their respective owners. A sword was considered an item of dress, and some swords were purely ornamental. Few men sat at a table on a long evening, however, fully armed.

"Sir Anthony," said Fletcher easily, "I am a thief, but I am no coward."

"Captain," said Sherwin, "if you will permit me, I want to confront this malevolent knight."

"My dear Sherwin," said the captain lightly, but with an air of skeptical concern, "do you intend to practice sword-play on this country man-at-arms?"

"If necessary," replied Sherwin.

The captain found this answer very amusing.

"The *Vixen* could use a seasoned knight whenever we board a prize," said Fletcher, when his quiet laughter was done. "Do try to spare this warrior's life long enough to convince him to join us—whether he wants to or not."

There was a long tradition of sailors and fighters alike being kidnapped, tied up, and hauled aboard a ship, where they accepted their new duties with a good grace or ill.

Sherwin felt a pitiless but undeniable thrill as the men from the *Vixen* filed from the room, leaving him to confront Sir Gregory.

Not only would he profit by Fletcher's wartime adventures, and by his own pen, putting silver into his own purse.

Sherwin could even elude the law if he did what he would like to do now—stab Sir Gregory through the heart.

23

"SIR GREGORY," said Sir Anthony, indicating Sherwin, "this is our guest, by way of the Inns of Court."

He pointedly did not offer Sherwin's name.

Sir Gregory gave a nod, as though he was well aware of the omission. "Are you consulting a youthful lawyer, then, Sir Anthony, to mend your troubles?"

"Actually, that's not a bad idea," said Sir Anthony with a puckish smile.

Katharine was out of sight, in another room. For all her aplomb and powers of communication, she had expressed the desire to set eyes on Gregory only when he was trussed and plucked—but Sherwin knew that she was overhearing every word. He could hear her feet whisper on the straw matting in the next room, and he had to believe that Sir Gregory could hear her, too.

"But I think you have had other guests this evening," said Sir Gregory, "in addition to this young lawyer dressed like a ship's soldier."

Sherwin was not prepared to like the man's character or bearing, and he did not. But the knight, who had been wounded in his right cheek at some point in the past, had the stance of an experienced fighter, steady on his feet and ready for whatever came.

He wore a heavy doublet of leather with high, padded shoulders, and tall boots. He carried a rapier at his left hip, and an elaborate dagger on his right, of the variety called a sword-breaker. Such weapons had deeply serrated blades. They were employed in the left hand and used to block or snatch rapier blades, and—sometimes—cause the slender blades to snap.

Another individual, one not introduced to Sherwin, lingered in the corner, out of the firelight, watching Sherwin as though he might prove to be a traveling conjurer, about to make a toad vanish. Sherwin gathered that this was the redoubtable Cecil.

"I am not here tonight to interrupt your feast," said Sir Gregory, prodding the goose carcass with his gloved hand.

He put the forefinger of his glove on the griffin-emblazoned wine mug Captain Fletcher himself had used, and Sherwin wondered how much such a man could guess. "I have received word of strangers on the land," continued the knight, "and I have ridden out to warn you."

"How thoughtful," said Anthony. "You are most kind, Sir Gregory."

"What sort of men are these supposed strangers?" asked

Sherwin, in an easy manner that sounded, to his own ears, entirely false.

"I know not," said Gregory. He looked Sherwin up and down, like a man sizing up a market-day ox. He seemed like a man accustomed to forceful statements, and not happy to be speaking to a putative lawyer from London.

"Do you suspect that the Spanish have positioned spies and agents on the coast," suggested Sherwin, "to tear down stiles and hedges, and prepare for an invasion?"

"I have just such a fear," said Gregory.

"Or are you concerned that some other strangely disposed travelers might have set foot here?"

"You guess too well," said Gregory.

"What do you suspect?" asked Sherwin.

"I suspect pirates," said Gregory.

"Oh, no, that is impossible," said Sir Anthony, no doubt sensing his great scheme dwindle to nothing.

By saying this, Sherwin knew, Sir Gregory had unwittingly forfeited any freedom he had. He had, moreover, ensured that a sea voyage was in his immediate future. No man who suspected pirates could be allowed to spread further rumors through Devonshire.

"You do not love Pevensey, Sir Gregory," said Sherwin, "and I do believe you would prefer a more rewarding duty under a more adventuresome master."

Gregory's next remark was nearly an admission that Sherwin was making accurate assumptions. It was a single syllable, voiced in a whisper. "Who?"

"Come with me," said Sherwin, "and find out."

Gregory was deeply puzzled, Sherwin reckoned, and resentful. He was also very interested.

"You can join a ship," said Sherwin, "that makes a man rich."

"And do what to win the money?" asked Gregory with a sullen stupidity Sherwin knew was false. Gregory was tempted.

Sherwin asked, "Are you so particular?"

"I am needed here," Gregory replied, in a tone that was regretful.

Sherwin could see that Gregory might have been a worthy acquaintance at some distant past, and might be again. His duties had coarsened him, and he was disillusioned.

"Why?" asked Sherwin. "So you can threaten maidens?"

He had not been prepared for the quick fury of this knight.

The man's rapier was instantly out of its sheath, and the point was touching Sherwin's throat.

Sherwin blinked, having to retrospectively imagine an event he had not actually perceived—the hand on the hilt, the breathtakingly fast flourish, the arm unbending, until it was locked at the elbow and the steel point an inch, or less, from Sherwin's power of speech.

"Who are you?" rasped Sir Gregory.

Sherwin had studied swordplay with a series of masters, all of them one-eyed, and sporting eye patches of various hues, as was common among such experts, and each with his own style of offense: the Genoan admiring the dagger, the Parisian swearing that only a footman would fight with anything but a single, elegant épée.

But the defensive maneuver proper when a blade was thrust against his throat was simple under any circumstances. Sherwin brushed the blade aside with his forearm, and grappled with his opponent, closing with him and striking him hard with the heel of his left hand, at the point of his chin.

The knight's head struck the edge of the table as he fell, and pewter dishes leaped and ran against each other.

Sir Gregory lay there in the firelight like an effigy.

He did not move.

VI

NO ALLY TO THE QUEEN

24

WHILE SHERWIN stayed behind to meet with Sir Gregory and his hulking companion, Fletcher and Highbridge had made their way quietly, quietly down a hallway. Sergeant Evenage and Bartholomew were entertaining themselves in a side room—the clink of wine cups was unmistakable as Evenage told the boy one of his sea tales.

Fletcher and his first officer went out into a back courtyard, paved with blue stone, where a young woman was setting out a dish for a cat.

Many houses had a kitchen built well apart from the main portion of the dwelling as a protection against possible fire, and this place was no exception. A walkway led to the building with wide-flung doors where an oven's fires were subsiding and a man with rolled-up sleeves and a heat-reddened face could be seen hanging a pot on a hook.

The young woman—a pretty lass—caught Captain

Fletcher's eye, and he stopped still as a bat made a trio of the cat and her mistress. The flying mouse almost collided with the stone wall of the kitchen, then angled upward.

The young woman caught sight of the creature and squealed, waving her hand at the pair of wings, as the cat looked up and then became momentarily rapt at the glimpse of a flying rodent flitting through the lingering July twilight.

The young woman noticed the two seamen. "I have no love for bats, good sirs," she said with a self-conscious laugh.

"And yet they have to find a living," suggested Fletcher gently, "out of the sky each night."

"Then, sir, let them hunt well away from me," she said.

Fletcher had to laugh, especially when the creature flitted and jerked over his own head, its compressed, enigmatic features impossible to gaze upon, it seemed to Fletcher, with anything like love.

"Molly," said the red-faced man, "come in from there."

But Fletcher put out his hand, and for an instant, out of courtesy or spontaneous affection, touched the young woman's hand.

"Have you ever considered a life on the sea?" asked Fletcher.

"Oh, sir!" exclaimed the young woman in wonder and alarm. There was another feeling, too, Fletcher sensed. She would not protest too greatly if Fletcher decided to free her from this place.

"Molly," persisted the man from the kitchen, "come here where I can see you."

He gave the two mariners a courteous nod, polite enough, knowing his master's visitors by reputation. But he was suspicious, too, and he closed the lower half of a stout double door, securing his daughter safely inside.

The cat—a long-legged gray tom—came over to rub its flanks against the captain's booted feet. Fletcher gave the creature a scratch between his ears. He could feel the scars under the cat's fur, claw marks from past seasons.

"I have been untruthful," he said.

"Have you, sir?" asked Highbridge.

"I don't want to avoid a fight with the Spaniards," said the captain, "simply because I am so gentle-hearted."

"No, sir?"

Fletched continued, "I'll risk my life, and yours, too, for a fortune. The truth is more blunt, Highbridge: I do not want to be an ally to the Queen."

Fletcher recalled vividly in that moment that he had once been sentenced to hang, and actually wore a noose of new hempen rope. He had been caught off Gravesend with a shipload of stolen iron, great ingots of the weighty metal, brute-heavy and hard to handle, but iron good enough to be made into cannons. For this Fletcher had been found guilty not only of piracy but also of interrupting the Queen's power to defend her realm—a species of treason.

He had climbed the stairs of the scaffold and stood as

the felonious charges proved against him were being read. Fletcher had been, although inwardly quailing, as prepared to die as was possible.

And then a messenger had appeared in the gold-and-crimson livery of the Queen's privy board of counselors, the Star Chamber, with a scroll bearing the Queen's seal impressed into sealing wax.

That evening in candlelight he had knelt in the presence of the red-wigged monarch as she made him a bargain he could not decline: she would grant his freedom for half of all that he ever took from any sea or port, from any English carrack or Arab dhow, any Dutch coracle or Spanish galleon.

No other mariner paid such a steep portion to Her Majesty. Fletcher, as her former controller, was in a position to know. Not Drake, not Hawkins, not Frobisher. And for this he had received no knighthood, no public acclaim. No pamphlets puffed up his name in the bookstalls of Saint Paul's, except to describe him as a felon.

"She is hungry, our Sovereign Lady Queen," said Fletcher now. "She is greedy, and I cannot forgive her."

"But she did offer you life these twenty years ago," said Highbridge, "and, sir, you took it."

"Highbridge, do you remember how you came to be my right-hand man?"

Highbridge rarely laughed out loud, but he had a warm smile. "I was fighting off half the crew of the *Jesus of Lubbeck*, Hawkins's old ship, near Southampton harbor.

They were drunk, and blasphemed in the presence of a lady. I complained civilly—"

"And you would have been killed if I had not stepped in. I hired you on the spot, did I not?"

"You said I would see high adventure and silver," said Highbridge, "if I followed you."

"I feel responsible for you, Highbridge, more than for all the others put together. You were the first of my crew, the cornerstone. If any harm should befall you, I would hate myself, and everything living. And I would never forgive our Sovereign Lady."

"Sir," said Highbridge, "there is the question of honor."

Fletcher made a hiss of impatience, a low, angry sound. "Do not speak to me, Highbridge, of honor. Does this tomcat know honor, or that pair of bat wings overhead?"

"Captain," offered Highbridge gently, "you are not a flying mouse."

"A pretty effort, this little protest of yours," said the captain with sudden force, "and one that fulfills your own sense of honor, I believe. But the truth is, Highbridge, I am an even greater rascal than people think me."

Highbridge turned away, rigid with suppressed concern. He could not meet his master's gaze. He spoke with a stiff deliberateness, choosing his words with care. "And do I understand, sir, that nothing I can say will make you change your mind?"

"I swear to you, Highbridge, I would sooner take up arms and fight on behalf of the Devil."

Highbridge looked upward and Fletcher followed his gaze. The bat had returned once again, tumbling ever higher, as if falling into the sky.

The captain put his arm on his old friend's shoulder. "I'll see you safe in some haven someday, Highbridge. With a cat named Hamm or Twill or some such, and a round fire to warm your boots. A cottage with a view of a river, Highbridge. And silver, Highbridge. Enough silver to buy—"

"To buy honor, Captain? I think honor cannot be bought."

"You are mistaken, old friend," said Fletcher with more weariness than anger. "Honor is bought daily, and for a cheap price, too."

But then Baines, the manservant who had served them dinner, hastened into the courtyard.

"My lords," he said, "I fear Sir Gregory has been killed!"

25

SHERWIN HAD NEVER USED the forearm block in actual fighting before, or the parry and subsequent blow that had proven alarmingly effective. He was shocked to see a vigorous adversary suddenly rendered harmless, stretched out with a vacant expression, the sort that only a lover should look down upon, a face empty of all misgivings.

Sherwin was sorry at this—something about the rough knight's spirit had been admirable, if not his character.

Sir Gregory's squire spoke to him anxiously and rubbed his limbs, and Sir Anthony called for his daughter. Katharine appeared from her side room and knelt across from the burly squire, pressing her fingers—gloveless and pale, Sherwin noted—against the pulse in the knight's neck.

"He breathes," she said. "And his heart is quick." She stood and gave Sherwin a look of conjecture. "Did you hit him with the butt of your pistol?"

"My lady," protested Sherwin, "I lifted only one hand against him."

Sir Gregory's squire walked over to Sherwin and stood facing him. Sherwin wished he had the talent of the Milanese tumblers he had seen at Smithfield Market one afternoon, a troupe of acrobats who could roll and leap, waging mock battles with dramatic fatal-looking falls, only to jump up again to thrilled applause.

Sherwin braced for the first blow, sure to be followed by another.

"My name is Cecil Rawes, sir," said the squire. "And I am ready to put out to sea."

Sherwin blinked in confusion, not understanding.

"I'll sail with you," added the squire, in an accent that helped to explain his long silences, a pronunciation so unusual that the words were hard to understand, a York-shire burr. "I'll sail a ship with you to put money into my poke, sir, if the ship will take me on."

At that moment the captain returned, and Bartholomew, the sergeant, and First Officer Highbridge with him.

"How dead is this country knight?" inquired the captain.

"Still alive, Captain," said Katharine.

Fletcher studied the unconscious knight briefly. "Not even half-dead," he said. "He'll return to health on board our ship."

"I'm not sending my daughter off to war," said Sir Anthony.

"My old friend," said Fletcher, "I shall avoid the fighting as I would avoid confession with a priest of Rome."

Sir Anthony reached for his walking stick and swung it like a sword, experimentally, aiming at nothing. He staggered, and had to catch himself from falling by clinging to Sherwin. "My health," he said, "will force me to stay here."

"Besides," said Fletcher in a sympathetic tone, "your absence would be suspicious, while Lord Pevensey will assume that your daughter was sent away for safety."

Sir Anthony gave a sharp, unhappy nod.

"She may be further out of harm," said the captain, in the tone of a man proposing a rabbit hunt, "with a shipload of brave Englishmen than she ever would be on this estate."

Sir Anthony bowed his head, silently conceding that Fletcher might be right.

"I know you, Captain, if you please, sir," said the squire, "by an engraving I saw in Winchester, in a broadside, *A Most Easy Guide to the Bloodiest Pirates of England.*" He spoke clearly so his accent might be understood. Sherwin knew the publication well, and thought it quite inferior work.

"What other pirates were there?" asked Fletcher.

"Only you, Captain Fletcher," said Cecil Rawes.

"There were surely others," said Fletcher in a tone of mild inquiry.

"There were going to be other printed sheets in the

series, sir," said the squire, "but the printer died, stabbed in a brawl."

"Killed by Drake's agents, would be my guess," said Fletcher, "keen to burnish his reputation."

"Go now," said Sir Anthony with a sob he could not hide. "Be quick, all of you, before I change my mind."

SIR GREGORY was put, still unconscious, into a wheelbarrow, and his squire rolled him along through the dark. The fields that Sherwin had first seen only that morning were now a deeply foreign land, and the road that had seemed welcoming was now cut and sliced with challenging ruts.

Baines followed with another wheelbarrow, one with a creaking wheel. The conveyance contained a small brass and leather trunk holding much of what Katharine would need during a short voyage, and all that necessity would allow her to bring on board the ship. Along with garments and an ivory comb, Katharine had placed into this chest a large banner, folded into a tidy, weighty triangle. She had told Sherwin that this was the griffin crest of her family, proof of the *Vixen*'s pacific intentions.

"Did you know, sir," Bartholomew asked Sherwin, "that there is a race of men without arms or legs that slithers along the Nile?"

"The anthrogastropods," said Sherwin. "I doubt such folk exist."

"Sergeant Evenage says he saw such a man," said Bartholomew, "a pickled corpse at Canterbury fair. His face was in his ribs, and his mouth opened directly to his stomach."

Katharine walked beside him, tearful at having taken leave of her father, and Sherwin did not feel that talk of armless, legless beings was what she needed to hear.

"Maybe someday, Bartholomew," said Sherwin, "you will be pickled, and on display at Smithfield. A Credulous and Innocent Manikin, Captured from His Pirate Lord."

"I doubt," said Bartholomew, "that you, sir, will allow that to happen."

WHEN HE WAS A BOY, farmland at night had always brought joy to Sherwin.

The withy gatherers would tie their small, lopsided vessels along the bank of the river during the summer darkness, and Sherwin had heard their voices, the soft conversation of men and women, brought across the fields with eerie clarity by the water.

Sherwin felt fortunate to possess a cheerful outlook regarding night, because the moon had been swallowed by cloud and an owl knifed the air overhead, a white-spanned hunter. Sherwin was undaunted. The trees, which had been entire nations of greenery and bird life by day, had retired into a dense darkness that, far from being reassuring, nevertheless seemed all the more wonderful with promise. The smells of the land, too, were rich and various: manure and fermenting hay, sap from recently split firewood, and the odor of field greens, timothy and sedge, drifting from the recently thatched roofs of Fairleigh's cottages.

The night had a quality of the unexplained for Sherwin, because he wondered if he would ever see such an hour on dry land again. He knew, as they took the road down to the sea cliff and made their way carefully along the sloping beach path, that the vessel waiting at the far edge of the high tide might be the conveyance that would bring him to the end of his life.

26

"CAPTAIN, I THOUGHT I'd have to send a shore party after you," said blond-bearded Lockwood. "The ship's been ready this hour past."

The *Vixen* was gently bucked and harried by the simmering tide, already high and beginning to ebb, as the same efforts that had careened the ship righted her again, so that her masts pointed unsteadily skyward.

She was hauled by the unified manpower of her crew down into the surf. Sherwin joined in, although Katharine and the captain and his first officer watched from nearby.

"No, sir, if you please," suggested the blond boatswain with a laugh, showing Sherwin how to put his weight on his back foot and lean with every ounce of his strength. Sherwin realized how relatively useless his help had been earlier that day.

The task was very nearly impossible at first. The boatswain broke into a song, and the men joined in, the *heave, oh, and heave oh*, sung in a rhythmic chant. Sherwin was nearly convinced that the ship was going to remain fixed to the shore—she was never going anywhere.

The waves were forceful, and the stones of the beach scraped the hull and gripped it as the ship shifted just slightly. No amount of effort would ever free this imposing but helpless vessel. The sweeps—the long oars that steadied the craft and could propel the ship—were put to desperate use, but no amount of straining and grinding of the oars was effective.

Or was it?

Sherwin and all the rest, including Katharine, climbed on board using a webbed rope ladder, with friendly assistance from their shipmates. Each time the surf surged under the keel, those oars levered the vessel outward, until at last, with a shiver, the rigging went taut and the masts straightened, and the ship was afloat.

The *Vixen* was alive in the water, but she was instantly pushed back, her keel barking against the sand. And even when she made her way out beyond the breakers, the current did not free her. Rocks began to approach on the larboard side, black stones that erupted beneath every wave, streaming with white and seeming sharper after each deluge.

Until the rocks looked smaller, through the darkness, the shore just a little more distant.

And they were truly under way.

KATHARINE LEANED OUT over the gunwale, gazing back at the shifting, night-shrouded cliffs of her home.

She had been on board ships before, several times, sailing with her father to Honfleur, delivering her father's investments in cooper's hoops and other goods and picking up spirits of cider. But for all her experience she had never voyaged on a warship before, and certainly not with a captain of such a belligerent reputation.

Katharine's initial impressions were of a ship of uncommon efficiency, with a soft-spoken officer in Highbridge, and seamen who were lively and dutiful. She was not so innocent as to allow herself to believe that the ship's company was as pacific as it appeared, but she felt no exceptional degree of apprehension.

She wore the ring her father had given her under her doeskin glove, and she could feel the cherished circlet now, pressing into her flesh as she gripped the ship's rail.

Trust him, her sister would have whispered.

Trust Sherwin.

But as for the captain, with his well-pronounced speech and his theatrical voice, Mary would have cautioned, *Trust him not so well.*

Her father had made his way to the top of the cliff, and now watched as the ship departed. She waved at him, and he waved in return, his hand a pale, indistinct trace through the salty air. Then she had to look away, too burdened by sorrow.

Katharine watched the ship's wake spreading landward through the dark. The unsettled water was itself a source of illumination. She saw more intensely than ever before that everything alive must indeed have an unknowable twin. This wake carrying the ship, that sailor clambering up the ratlines, and certainly that captain breathing on his hands to keep them warm. Each had an invisible shadow, a double that could not be perceived.

Sherwin joined her.

"How long, do you think," she asked, "before I see Fairleigh again?"

Her question was not idle. The thoughtfulness, and frankness, of his answer would be further proof that he merited her faith.

"I have been asking myself the same question," he said.

"Someday you might love the place the way I do," she said.

"I admired your father, and the fine house, and the fertile fields," he said. "And the brave goose, if you will permit me. Although, if you forgive me, my lady, your estate suffers only the very minor flaw of not possessing a river."

"It has one," she protested with a laugh. "Not a wide river, but one with grassy banks and its share of moorhens. I played on it, and I learned to handle a boat, too."

"Pardon me, I did not know," said Sherwin.

She laughed again. Despite her sadness at parting from her father, she found Sherwin a more than pleasurable companion.

"What is the name of your grand river, Lady Katharine?"

"Well, it doesn't have much of a name. We call it the Ooze."

Sherwin gave a polite cough. "Forgive me, but I think your river deserves a more beautiful appellation, Katharine."

"Does it indeed?" she asked, in an air of good-humored challenge.

He ducked his head self-consciously as he added, "A name as charming, if you will allow me, as the people who live there, and the lady who graces the place."

Katharine felt her father's absence all the more keenly now, and wondered: Would Sherwin be someone who could ease her distress at departing? He had a warm smile, it was true, and a winning way of seeming both shy and forthright at once.

"Do you have any particular friend in your life, Sherwin?" she asked.

"Any particular friend?" asked Sherwin, as though slow to understand what she might mean. "You mean, perhaps, any exceptional companion among the ladies."

"You guess my meaning well, Sherwin."

"In truth," he said, with an undeniable warmth to his gaze, "I have no special claim upon my heart." He added, as though reluctant to offend, but keen to understand, "If that is what you mean."

"That," she said, "is exactly what I mean."

"And as for you," he asked, "what gentleman of this pretty countryside has earned your affections?"

"No one," she said.

She could not deny it—he gave a happy smile at this reassurance. And he added, "This, for me, comes as very welcome tidings."

She could not suppress her happiness—she liked Sherwin very much.

27

THE DARK WATERS of the English Channel were battered by a strong wind out of the west.

Foam shot through the air, and streaking brine spent itself against the reefed and inclined canvas of the sails.

Katharine's presence on board was explained by telling the truth. The crew was told that she was the owner of a ship that the *Vixen* was setting sail westward to intercept. Highbridge murmured something about keeping the cargo "out of the hands of creditors," and the crew responded with knowing and sympathetic smiles.

Her presence also helped solidify Sherwin's role aboard the vessel. If there had been any doubt whether he would bring good luck or bad, Katharine was evidence of a turn toward respectability—even gentlefolk had to resort to cunning. His solicitousness toward Katharine, and the way she smiled at him, made the crew members feel that the ship had taken on a courtly quality, with a role to play in the financial and perhaps even the romantic future of a gentleman and a lady.

Sir Gregory and Cecil were lodged with the master gunner, and Sir Gregory accepted his new condition as a potential sea warrior with a grudging grace. Possible sea strife against the Spanish was, after all, a chance at honor and gold. Although the knight was troubled by sea-sickness, he and Cecil were kept busy helping the gunner clean and repair a variety of weapons, and ready the mortars, muskets, and other firearms for battle.

For his part, Sherwin sharpened rapiers and pikes with a whetstone, and when he was not busy sharpening steel he was busy kneading hoof-oil into leather. Every boot and belt, strap and scabbard became instantly stiff because of the salt air, unless worked on regularly.

What might be a simple task on land became a constant effort against the bucking, tossing progress of the ship and the extreme slant of the ship as she tacked against the gusty and variable weather. The youngest sailors were sent aloft to take in or pay out canvas, as required, and even the most experienced seaman sometimes had to cling to a rope to keep from falling all the way across the deck.

The quartermaster, a mariner named Grewel, was a short, balding man with responsibilities over goods and ballast stored within the ship. He called the strongest seamen to help rearrange the cargo in the hold as the vessel's interior shifted. Cecil Rawes helped, and so did Sherwin and the sergeant, along with other able men, moving sea chests and barrels into new positions.

"Not a sign of that old leak, Mr. Highbridge," called out Grewel.

"Thank God for that," breathed Evenage.

THE NIGHT was still murky during a quiet respite from the strong winds, dawn yet hours away, when a howl rose from belowdecks, sharpening to a scream.

Sherwin looked around for Katharine, and she was there beside him, gloved and mantled, her features hidden by her hood.

"Our shipmate Tryce," explained Sherwin. "Dr. Reynard is working to save his life."

"May God steady the surgeon's hand," said Katharine.

"Will you be comfortable in your berth?" asked Sherwin, trying to make easy conversation over the wailing from the surgeon's quarters.

"Captain Fletcher has knocked together a cabin for me beside his in the sterncastle," she said. Ships had rooms and quarters of variable sizes, all small and capable of being taken down and rearranged quickly. Accommodating a lady, or any unexpected visitor, was no particular challenge to the carpenter and his mates. "I've been helping our shipmates by making an inventory."

"An inventory of what?" asked Sherwin.

"I'll be mending and cleaning linen to be used as slings and bandages, to ease the suffering of the wounded—should there be any. Mr. Highbridge suggested the task, and I am happy to help."

Sherwin realized how startled Katharine felt, to be so suddenly at sea, and as troubled by the sudden silence as she must have been by the screams. Tryce had seemingly succumbed to oblivion as the surgeon's apprentice carried a bundle from belowdecks and padded solemnly to the ship's rail.

A splash followed, the sound muffled by the wind—Tryce's limb was offered to the deep.

She said, "No doubt you are well accustomed to shipboard suffering."

Sherwin had to laugh. "No, I'm new to this life."

He told her then of the sinking of the *Patience*, and of his own plunge into the cold sea. By the time his tale was completed, the *Vixen* had left the rocky shoreline well behind.

"For me," he concluded, with perhaps a dollop of heavy drama, "the sea is the source of torment."

"How fine, Sherwin," said Katharine, "to have survived such adventures."

Sherwin had not viewed his near misfortunes in quite that dashing perspective. But he liked the way it sounded. He allowed himself a brief vision, an actor portraying him, giving voice to a speech. *Nature that alloyed us from four elements.* Not a bad beginning, thought Sherwin.

Something, something. He would have to write all this down. *The sweet climb from brine to comradely smiles.* The scansion needed planing, like knots in a timber, but the captain had been right. Surely this beautiful new friend would inspire him to write the sort of verses that were bound to be declaimed to the admiration of the plumed and perfumed as well as the penny-payers.

He imagined the actor depicting Sherwin Morris, late of Her Majesty's Privateer Fleet, drawing a sword and taking a stand.

Against a rampant pig.

"They were not adventures, actually," he said, in a tone of self-admonishment, "so much as awkward misfortunes."

AS DAWN BROKE, herring gulls followed in the ship's wake, hungry and assertively curious, wheeling and bickering with a freedom it gave Sherwin pleasure to watch.

The seas were too rough for regular gunnery practice, but the four falconets—light cannon—on deck were each loaded and fired once, the brass guns erupting in puffs of smoke that streamed instantly away in the wind.

The master gunner was a man named Ralph Aiken, a small individual who stood with his arms folded as the sergeant spoke loudly into his ear. "We have enough shot for one rehearsal with the matchlocks, do we not?"

The matchlocks, a variety of musket, had been oiled and polished by Sir Gregory and Cecil, under the instructing gaze of the master gunner. Sir Gregory and Cecil looked on from a distance now, eager to see the success of their efforts.

"No, not so much gunpowder as to permit a single

proper mock skirmish," said Aiken emphatically. "But to please you, sergeant, and our young gentleman, I'll spare a spoonful of black powder, just one, to give him the feel of the weapon."

"The gunner's been as deaf as a bucket," Evenage confided to Sherwin, "ever since a murder piece blew up in his face against the Turks off Joppa." A *murder piece* was a cannon used in close-quarter combat.

The sergeant used a leather powder flask to prime the weapon as the master gunner looked on, pursing his brow when a trace of the powder spilled.

"Easy, there, easy," the gunner chided.

"We're low on lead shot, and powder, too," murmured Evenage. "From what I hear, the Spaniards have bought up every ounce of spare shot metal in Europe."

Evenage showed Sherwin how to fit a matchlock musket onto a tripod and aim the weapon out over the tossing waves. The coiled fuse smoked and smoldered. Sherwin triggered the firearm, and breathed the brief, eye-smarting whiff of the discharge. The amount of powder they had put into the weapon had been small, and so the report was lost in the rumble of the sails as the luff—the weather edge of the canvas—lost the wind and found it again.

Evenage prepared Sherwin in other ways, too, explaining that bomboes, as he called them, could be set alight and hurled into the face of an enemy. These were iron balls stuffed with flammable cloth—called bombast—along with soft wax and gunpowder, all topped off with a fuse.

Each iron bomb weighed more than a pound, and hurling one any distance would be a challenge. "One of these," said Sherwin, "would be as dangerous to the man throwing it as it would be to his enemy."

"Of that, sir," said the sergeant, with a brisk cheerfulness—as though mayhem was both inevitable and regretted—"there can be but little doubt."

Sir Gregory joined them. He had, willingly or not, signed on for a percentage of the ship's earnings, and would be as well compensated as Sherwin. His financial prospects, and his chance at glory, apparently did much to assuage his chagrin at being captured. He appeared, in fact, to be willing to adapt to this new life, practicing now with the butt of an arquebus, hammering down a phantom opponent.

He glanced at Sherwin and offered, "The time I had to kill a man with one of these, this is how I did it." Sir Gregory was putting on a show of masculine vigor, but his cheeks were hollow.

"Ah," said Sherwin, trying to appear occupied with his pistol—without daily polishing, it was true, it became tarnished.

Sir Gregory gave Sherwin a challenging smile, and asked, "How about you, lad?"

"Surely," said Sherwin, trying to make a joke of the conversation, "you are not offering to kill me?"

"No, I've forgiven you your triumph over me, for as long as we are shipmates," replied Sir Gregory. His words were polite enough, but his tone was hard and dismissive. "Tell me," insisted Sir Gregory, "how many men have you slain?"

"My master, Sir Gregory," joined in Bartholomew, "killed a hundred in one day."

"River smelt, that is," said Sherwin with a laugh. Indeed, the net fishing on the upper Thames had been rewarding, and the fried fish delicious.

"Well," said Sir Gregory, with a dry laugh, "perhaps soon you will have your chance."

28

FOR TWO ENTIRE DAYS and nights the *Vixen* tacked westward, sailing hard against the wind. The vessel labored her way past the west country port of Plymouth, her decks awash with water, compelled westward by the desire to intercept the *Rosebriar*.

Sir Gregory came on deck again a few times, only to fall down, and Lockwood and his mates had to seize the knight and hang on to keep him from washing overboard in the heavy seas that increasingly punished the vessel.

Sherwin spent time on the quarterdeck, clinging to a rail and shivering, soaked through his heavy mantle, as the captain took no great effort in keeping his own balance.

"When you are wealthy," sang out the captain, "dear Sherwin, when you are happily rich from writing about my life, not to mention from your portion of our prizes, you can pay mariners to breathe in this wet salty air. You will smirk to yourself how dry you are in some lady's chamber, lace upon your sleeve."

"I wish the day would hasten," acknowledged Sherwin.

"When you decide which actor should portray me in your rhyming epic," said Fletcher, "make sure he resembles me in leg and bearing, but he should be younger."

Salt water flying through the air stung Sherwin as he answered, "But surely a younger man could don a gray wig, sir, and learn to speak as you do."

"Yes, but I want to live on as a younger man, year after year kept in life's springtime by you." He asked, meaningfully, "Have you any new ones?"

"Sir?"

"New verses regarding me."

"A few," said Sherwin, "but they are sparse."

"Speak them to me now."

Sherwin blinked against the salt spray and recited,

> "But had life no date, and wish no need,
> You would not treasure
> What my quill could breed.
> You would be golden, free from all decay,
> And your unfaded spirit
> Freshen dusk each day."

Fletcher considered and at last gave a thoughtful laugh. "All too smooth, Sherwin, and too philosophical. Fire is what the penny-payers demand. Give them fire."

But Sherwin wondered if the subjects of mortality

and ambition were too close to the truth for Captain Fletcher's pleasure.

SHERWIN PAID a visit to Tryce, whose stump was bandaged in clean crasko linen, the sort used for towels and surgeons' bindings. Sherwin was aware that Katharine was the person to thank for such fresh surgical dressing.

"Did you dine on my leg," Tryce asked, "in the gentlemen's quarters?"

"No, we had mutton and herring," said Sherwin, "and wine as red as your blood, though not as brave."

"Oh, you gentlefolk," said Tryce with a weak sneer. "Always shaping words to do the duty of a manly deed."

But he put his hands out to soften any offense his manner might cause, taking Sherwin by the arm before he departed the crowded, creaking hole of a surgeon's den.

"Don't fear for the captain's ship, sir," said Tryce. "She's the finest I've ever sailed. If she has to claw off the shore against a furacane, she can." *Furacanes* were the spinning storms of the West Indies, notoriously destructive.

Sherwin smiled. He appreciated the reassurance, but he had the bleak certainty that Tryce would not survive to see many more mornings.

KATHARINE WAS SUFFERING from sea-sickness and kept to her cabin. Sherwin missed her companionship very much, and marveled at his own luck at possessing— quite by good luck—a mariner's constitution.

With the sea far above the vessel one instant, and plunging far below the next, so that the bottom fell out of the world in a feeling like sick drunkenness, Sherwin could not be surprised at the sight of Cecil Rawes bawling into a bucket or Sir Gregory too feeble to crawl upon the deck before he spewed empty heaves.

Highbridge caught Sherwin's sleeve as the two of them clung to the manrope down the center of the deck.

"Speak to the captain of honor," Highbridge called into Sherwin's ear. "Say how much you look forward to setting eyes on the Spaniards fleeing English waters, and how much you love your country."

Sherwin, who had no doubt the *Vixen* would battle the Spaniards if duty and necessity demanded, did as Highbridge suggested, and in response the captain only shook his head and gave a dry laugh. "Honor," he said, "was the first word Highbridge learned to gum as an infant."

SHERWIN, wet to the skin, dried out happily over a brazier of sea coals in the soldiers' quarters, and consoled Sir Gregory and Cecil that no one died of the spinning gyres the ship was describing, sailing, as it seemed, down a whirlpool.

Evenage waxed his belt and oiled his pistol, and spoke of the demon of Ely, a naked, biting creature caught by a bishop and hung up in a cage—a tiny devil dropped from his master's pocket one All Saints' Eve. For his part,

Bartholomew juggled pistol balls, dark, shining orbs like stone eyes, and he could make them vanish, too, to the worried amazement of Cecil.

"What scamp taught you that?" asked the squire.

"Ah," said Bartholomew with an air of nostalgia striking in a child, "my former master taught me more wonders than this."

JUST BEFORE DAWN on the fourth day out, the cry *sail-ho* sang from the lookout.

A warship was the lightning rumor throughout the ship.

Every human being who was able crowded the deck, pointing and exclaiming as they caught sight of her, her furled sails now visible, now eclipsed by a wave the size of Canterbury Cathedral.

Only after a long moment of patient coaxing by the captain did Sherwin see a flash of anything dark and solid enough to be a vessel. She appeared and vanished—naked masts, a stern galley painted red and black, the vessel heeling with the west wind.

Or that was what he thought he saw—she was a glimpse too fleeting to be certain. And the early dawn was still too dark. Shipmates speculated among themselves, loudly enough to be heard from the quarterdeck.

She was the *Ark Royal*, Lockwood guessed, Lord Howard's flagship. Howard was Lord of the Admiralty, and in charge of coordinating Her Majesty's naval defenses. Sherwin gathered that no one on the *Vixen* wanted to encounter the admiral, and he had a fairly good idea why.

If the Crown was becoming disillusioned with Captain Fletcher, or if the admiral, on his own initiative, decided to examine Fletcher's accounts, the ship and its cargo could be impounded, along with each crew member's share.

No, it was not the admiral's vessel after all, Lockwood surmised at length. Then she was surely the *Dainty*, Hawkins's ship, or a ship packed with gunpowder, made to look alive and manned but waiting for the Armada to draw near, so it might explode and kill two shiploads, or three—or a dozen—of the Spanish intruders.

Or perhaps it was a Spanish decoy, a hulk crammed with gunpowder meant to seduce an unwary privateer.

29

THE STERN LIGHTS of what turned out to be an English vessel swung before them through the stirring dawn.

She was the *Roebuck*, a ship owned by the courtier and poet Sir Walter Raleigh, and captained by Sir John Burgh. The *Vixen* drew alongside, and the sea fell and filled, the rigging of the two vessels close to tangling.

"Good Captain Fletcher," called Captain Burgh through a speaking trumpet made of brass, the metal gleaming in the hint of morning light. "What a pleasure it is to see you! Lord Howard said Her Majesty could not rely on you, but I told his lordship you were an Englishman to the bone."

Sherwin was proud to hear Captain Burgh's approving, if optimistic, opinion of Fletcher's allegiance.

Fletcher accepted a speaking trumpet of his own from a seaman. He put the instrument to his lips, looking like a man called upon to play a tune and happy to do his best.

Sherwin recognized that any occasion that involved talking pleased Captain Fletcher well.

"You are generous," called Captain Fletcher in return, "in your estimation of my devotion. But tell me—where is Hawkins now?"

"Captain Hawkins is many leagues to the west, off Scilly," came the response. "But Lord Howard himself will be sailing these waters soon, God willing," said Burgh. "I will be pleased to tell him of the eager spirit of your brave crew."

Sherwin was aware that Captain Burgh might well be one of Fletcher's admirers, but he might also be gifted in subtle manipulation. Sherwin was also conscious of how vast the waters were, and how few the sea captains with enough experience to defend them.

Sergeant Evenage said, to no one in particular, "I fear the Lord Admiral would just as soon see us hang like cats."

The captain of the *Roebuck* put his hand to his ear in a pantomime of deafness as the wind rumbled through the furled sails of both vessels, and for the moment Fletcher made no additional remark.

"Have you seen any sign," came the question at last from Burgh, "of the Armada?"

The crew of the *Vixen* stirred. They were troubled by this indication of ignorance on the part of a captain who was in a position to know.

"We had to put to shore for repairs," explained Fletcher, "and we know but little."

Burgh was authentically unable to hear this last remark, and Fletcher repeated the statement all the more clearly, in the tones of a man who in years past had addressed the Admiralty regarding the cost of everything from spun hemp to spruce-wood masts.

The captains knew well that everyone aboard both vessels heard every word and so they spoke as diplomats might, or as cordial but circumspect lawyers. The crew of the *Vixen*, it was clear to Sherwin, loyally supported Fletcher, but it was also apparent, judging by the looks of determination, that the thought of fighting the Spanish gave no one any qualms.

"No ships," called Captain Burgh, "aside from Drake's fleet, have come from the west these last several days."

He paused to let this message penetrate, like a town crier with important and complex tidings.

Then he added, "Our own warships are trapped in Portsmouth by this wind and only work their way out slowly. A scattering of sentry ships mans the Channel, and we are pleased that you have joined us."

Fletcher turned his head as a spray of salt water drenched him.

"Does the Armada even exist?" he called. The speaking trumpet made his voice piercing and metallic. "I have doubted King Philip's fighting spirit all this while."

He had to ask the question twice, word for word, and the answer was a laugh, followed by, "I fear it is true. The Spanish have taken refuge in ports all along the way."

Fletcher did not seem to notice as still another upsurge of water soaked him. The seas lifted high and fell away again, and the *Vixen* dropped momentarily far below the level of the *Roebuck*, only to be swelled skyward again as the seas grew heavier by the instant.

"How many," called Fletcher, "ships do the Spanish have?"

"One hundred, by some estimates," was the answer, "or even more, with dozens further in the Low Countries, under the command of the Duke of Parma. They have galleons and galleasses, along with urcas and merchant ships packed with soldiers."

The crew of the *Vixen* stirred, excited and dismayed at this confirmation.

"But," added Captain Burgh, "the Armada has vanished."

Sherwin was quietly amazed to hear this, and the crew members around him jostled each other.

Fletcher shook his head privately, unhappy at the news, or skeptical.

"Are you well supplied," came Burgh's query through the wind, "with shot and powder?"

Highbridge made a questioning sign to the master gunner. Aiken inclined his head confidingly toward the first officer, knowing what was being asked without perceiving the words.

Sherwin could hear him clearly: "Enough for two or three days' steady fighting."

The captain passed along this estimate to the captain of

the *Roebuck*, and the response was, "We have a limited supply ourselves—I pray it proves enough."

THE TWO SHIPS PARTED, the *Vixen* tacking her way westward, the *Roebuck* lying to, enduring the bucking seas by remaining across the wind.

Highbridge stood close to the captain, murmuring into his ear. Sherwin thought he could read the entreaty on the first officer's lips. Fletcher looked away with that characteristic falcon stare, gazing everywhere but into the eyes of another man.

When she had nearly vanished beneath the horizon, the *Roebuck* turned into the wind, a shape like a fly on the gray seas, sailing haltingly in the *Vixen*'s wake.

"Highbridge," said Captain Fletcher, for all to hear, "order up red wine for every man, double rations."

The featured beverage on most vessels was beer or cider. But a privateer enjoyed the spoils of shipping from around the world, and the men were cheered by this welcome revitalization. Red wine, furthermore, was thought to strengthen the liver, the seat of courage.

And courage, thought Sherwin, was what they would all soon require.

THAT EVENING Sherwin joined Fletcher and Highbridge in the captain's cabin.

The cabin had tall, narrow windows, like those of a tall, narrow London house, and beyond the windows the sea was agitated, fuming in the wake of the *Vixen*. An assembly of strongboxes, with large black locks, was secured under a table, and the cabin wall was partly adorned with an arras, a hanging screen against a bulkhead.

The arras was decorated with the depiction of a ship sailing into a harbor, protected by a benevolent figure twice the size of the vessel, half-submerged in the water. This giantess or goddess was a modestly attired female form, extending one hand to shield the vessel, as it seemed, from the rays of the sun.

The captain poured Sherwin a mug of wine. "Or," asked the captain, "will you have brage, Highbridge's drink of choice?"

Sherwin liked brage—ale laced with honey and spices— but decided it was more politic to enjoy the same beverage as Captain Fletcher.

The three of them sat in the shivering lamplight. The smell of the burning candles was sharp—expensive tallow, but smoky. The drinking cups and candle holder were kept from sliding to the floor by fiddles—detachable rails fixed around the edge of the table.

Highbridge could not hide a benevolent, even satisfied, smile. "Our gunners need no practice," he was saying. "Nor will our guns burst—we put those new sakers to use against the *Santa Catalina*."

One of the reasons for gunnery practice was to see that the ordnance was sound—bursting weapons were a cause of many fatalities.

"I recollect our combat with that ship," said the captain, "with no pleasure."

"And our repairs are holding—we suffer not a single leak," said Highbridge.

"All the more reason," said the captain dryly, "to smash our ship to toothpicks."

Highbridge laughed. Sherwin had never seen him so lighthearted. The first officer excused himself and left the cabin for the wet, tumultuous conditions on deck.

"Highbridge and I agree, Sherwin," said the captain, "that we are on a course to kiss the Devil."

"Sir?"

"Where the *Rosebriar* is expected to appear," said Fletcher, "and where I fear the Spanish are hiding, are in the same vicinity on the charts."

"Where is that, sir?"

"Off that Cornish promontory called the Lizard."

Sherwin was too excited by this news to say anything for the moment.

Fletcher pulled at his lower lip thoughtfully for a moment. Then he added, "When you write the play, *Fletcher and His Ship Part Hell and Win Enduring Peace in Triumph*, make sure some tall youth portrays Highbridge. Some dark, frank man of strength, acting as my conscience."

"Is it true that we will fight the Spanish, sir?" asked Sherwin.

He did not want the hour to arrive—but the fear drew him in at the same time, an enthralling dread.

"Fight them?" asked Fletcher, as though the question surprised him. Then he gave a sad laugh. "Sherwin, we may have no choice."

VII

ARMADA

30

THE SUN was an unsteady presence the following morning, the twentieth day of July.

The cry from aloft that dawn had a different quality from that of any human voice Sherwin had ever heard, a shrill of marvel and apprehension.

"There," cried the lookout once again, like a man driven to the point of mania. "There, off the starboard bow!"

The deck was instantly thronged with shipmates, who stood observing the seas to the west. There was nothing there—no ship in sight.

A mist had risen to the west, in response, perhaps, to the rising of the sun, and the sea, easier in its temperament, remained sullen. Katharine joined Sherwin with the captain on the quarterdeck, but the captain was the only individual on the deck who did not strain to see what was hidden through the haze.

He seemed to know what was beyond already, or perhaps he had seen enough at a glance to be able to infer all the rest.

The sea was a wrinkling, unwrinkling expanse, and it met the blurred ether of gray that descended from the sky, and not so much as a floating spar marred the ocean's surface.

And then a ship appeared, a craft with angled sails, her canvas being shaken out as the blustery gale faded and lost strength.

She was a pretty ship, the sort built for speed and maneuverability—an urca, as Sherwin knew from his wharfside haunts, watching Canary wine being delivered. This solitary craft was a foreign ship, almost certainly Spanish, but so elegant in her lines and peaceful in her manner that Sherwin felt his shipmates around him relax.

The mist lifted further, and another vessel joined the first—a galleass, a low-cut, cunning ship, familiar to Sherwin only from tavern woodcuts.

The sight of this second vessel was less reassuring than the first, in Sherwin's eyes, but she likewise looked pacific in intent. She was so appealing as she spread her canvas, catching the milky sunlight, that Sherwin could believe that no harm would ever fall upon anything living.

At the sight of a third vessel, a galleon larger than the *Vixen* bearing down past the two smaller craft, the crew around Sherwin turned to their battle stations without a murmur of command.

The vision that was about to reveal itself was anticipated by everyone aboard the ship, and as the haze was diluted, moment by moment, the pricking out of one more ship, and then another, took place like the careful hand of a seamstress piercing a certain but invisible pattern.

Galleons worked their way into a ragged line ahead of merchant vessels that wallowed low in the water, the cargo ships no doubt heavy with fighting men and arms. The smaller urcas and galleasses sped ahead of the others in the fleet, finding water unbroken by any wake.

ONE HUNDRED SHIPS, and more.

Every observable vessel of the still-far-distant Armada set her sails and aimed her course directly at the sudden English interloper.

Fletcher was intent, but as yet made no sign of apprehension. He gave a quiet command to Highbridge, and soon footsteps pounded belowdecks, and the ship resounded with the sound of gun carriages, a chorus of groans and squeals as the artillery was swabbed and primed in the bowels of the ship.

The armorer's store of weapons chimed somewhere belowdecks as mariners were outfitted with pikes and short swords, able-bodied seamen reappearing on deck with the look of an anxious but determined fighting force. Lockwood thrust a short-ax through his belt, and Sir Gregory appeared carrying a tongue-of-beef halberd, stabbing the air experimentally with a look of intense satisfaction. Evenage wore an iron corselet and sported a helmet, a handsome gleaming piece of armor with a metal crest.

But the captain had the air of an astronomer trying to descry his favorite planet. He gazed long at the Armada as the vapor lifted and the entire fleet became visible. This quiet abstraction on the part of the captain gave Sherwin to believe that the *Vixen* was in preparation for battle only as a precaution.

Sherwin was startled when Fletcher called for Katharine, not in a tone of voice of Sherwin had heard before.

The captain was suffused with emotion.

He ordered Katharine to come to his side, and pointed out across the water to indicate the sight of a single burning ship that, in a fleet of warships, caused him the greatest consternation.

Within moments, Katharine was in tears.

"Is that your ship?" asked the captain, a voice tight with fury. "Is that the *Rosebriar*, with our treasury of cinnamon bark?"

Katharine could only nod and give a breathless "I fear so."

31

A SLURRY OF SMOKE rising from a pack of ships showed where a vessel had been taken as a prize and set alight—and her cargo either wasted or plundered and the ship scuttled.

But there was no time after the discovery of the loss for any financial or emotional inventory. As Sherwin stood comforting Katharine, the sea around them altered.

One instant the gray water was restless and shifting, with the Armada standing clear as an imposing backdrop, an impending but still-distant threat. The next moment several more vessels were so close that the figures of sailors and soldiers could be seen, and the far-off naval tapestry had new dimensions, texture, and depth.

The wind was stirring after a brooding respite, and the rigging sang a low, solemn warning. The originally sighted urca and galleass drew near, followed by a wedge of vessels, and behind that advance the entire Armada bulked all the closer to the *Vixen*.

After the tense but ultimately benevolent contact with

the *Roebuck*, Sherwin was expecting a parley, perhaps at most a warning shot, followed by Fletcher buying time as his crew set the sails for a swift departure eastward.

This hope was punctured somewhat when the captain said, "Katharine, step into my cabin, if you please, and take your ease there for the duration." He added, "Don't despair about your ship, my lady—if we are stubborn and Spanish gunnery incompetent, we may salvage a good deal of treasure yet."

He said this as a man might discuss gammon to accompany his ale, in a distracted, easy tone that gave no hint of what was about to come. Katharine did not take his advice at once, seeming both shaken and hopeful at his remarks. Fletcher shot a glance toward Sherwin and said, "You don't intend to enter battle naked, do you, friend?"

Naked, in a military sense, meant unarmed. Bartholomew was at Sherwin's side at once, carrying what looked like the iron cast of half a man. A battle corselet was fitted over Sherwin, opening and closing like a book around him. Buckles were fastened, and Sherwin felt like the grand tortoise he had seen at the Smithfield bestiary, a large tub of a creature with sleepy reptilian eyes and an appetite for watercress.

"If I fall into the water," said Sherwin, "I'll sink straight to the bottom." His voice had a bronze resonance, and he could not keep from enjoying the heroic tenor of his accent as he added, in an attempt at humor, "I shall battle the giants of the deep."

"Hush, sir," protested Bartholomew. "Speak of dire events, and they are sure to happen."

WITHOUT ANY PROTOCOL, with no warning or opportunity to reflect or pray, the urca vanished behind a cloud of white smoke, and a cannon shot skipped across the water. We're still too far apart, thought Sherwin. The distance was so great that the artillery had been comically ineffective, like a market-day brawl just half in earnest.

But it could only be seen as abruptly impolite, this first shot, not so much a warning as an attempt to test the range. The report of the cannon was muted by distance but was a metallic, percussive punch in the belly nonetheless, and to his surprise Sherwin smelled the smoke in the next instant.

He caught a brief snatch of Spanish language, *Madre de díos* carried on the wind—harsh, musical, and surprising. Another voice called, from the arriving galleass, and behind them a galleon, at the head of a flotilla of her companions, was growing huge against the rest of the approaching force.

The *Vixen* was going to be wedged in after only a few more heartbeats, and Sherwin looked at the captain, sure the order would come for the vessel to turn about.

"Steady on, Highbridge," said Fletcher, fastening his mantle about him like a man in the theater pits, settling in for an hour of entertainment. He glanced at Sherwin with a further comment: "If we turn and flee now, we'll never get our hands on so much as a stick of our precious cargo."

Katharine was still at Sherwin's side; before she left, she did something that stirred him as much as the line of attack descending on the *Vixen*. She put her lips to Sherwin's, kissed him, and said, in a shaken whisper, "You are my heart."

This statement struck Sherwin all the more fully because of the expectation that soon the parts of bodies—limbs, bones, and for all he knew actual hearts—might be strewn about him.

She was gone then before he could respond, and he was left trying to pull together a fragment of poetry in response—all he wanted to do was sink into a safe, quiet place beside her.

A swivel gun fired from the approaching galleass, and Evenage called to Sherwin, "Quickly, sir, if you will," and Sherwin hurried to the gun mounts on the deck, taking the matchlock he was given by Bartholomew and settling the firearm onto its support.

The captain murmured something to Highbridge, and the officer spoke to Lockwood. The boatswain's whistle piped, and to Sherwin's surprise the ship made no move to turn about and flee east with the strong west wind—the same force that compelled an entire Spanish navy closer, so close they would be in easy cannon range soon.

Very soon.

Sherwin had a muted sense of what the captain might have in mind: if the *Vixen* could lance through the parting mass of the Armada and reach the site of the burning cargo ship, she could cut what remained of the *Rosebriar* out of the fleet and guide her toward the open sea. This was a desperate hope, and such an attempt was carrying a lust for wealth to an extreme. No amount of possible reward, in Sherwin's view, made such a risk remotely desirable.

The wind behind the Spanish grew more forceful, driving the urcas and the galleons together. The ships were close to colliding, and within the fleet some did grind together, the sound like doors slamming. Sherwin had the impression that the enemy fleet was on a long slope, sliding down an incline. That accounted for the relentless momentum behind them, and for the virtual silence. Sherwin told himself that he needed more time before he started to kill people—or to die.

He was not prepared. And when more ordnance was fired—the Spanish gunners seeming to have as much enthusiasm as gunpowder—he was relieved at how wide of the mark the shots were, too far short, too far aft.

Bartholomew was putting up screens so sparks and splinters from either side would not distract Sherwin during the fight to come. A shot hit the side of the *Vixen*—a single, round reverberation that made Sherwin jump.

Evenage was unseen, on the other side of the woven partition, and the sergeant said, "Hold on to something, sir."

A simple command that, under the circumstances, made little sense.

"Sir," urged Bartholomew, "please set your feet and hang on."

32

THERE WAS NOTHING to hang on to, and no immediate need, as far as he could see.

In truth, however, Sherwin could see very little aside from the chased brass of his firearm, because of the smoke from the Spanish guns flowing through the wind. The gunports of the *Vixen* rattled and clattered belowdecks, the vibration of the wooden shutters traveling through the vessel.

He knew what it portended, and how vulnerable a ship was with her gunports, so close to the waterline, gaping open. He felt the ship shift subtly as the guns were shoved out through the ports, ready to fire. And yet Sherwin still felt that some reprieve might be enjoyed, that the mood might change once more, and the entire exercise fall to bluffing and gesturing, no one really about to be hurt.

Then the staggered explosions shocked Sherwin and made it hard for him to breathe, as a cloud of yellow and green smoke filled the air and seared his lungs, and he was instantly all but deaf. He did set his feet, then, too late, after he had nearly fallen.

Tears flowed down his cheeks, his eyes burning with the smoke. As the fumes were torn away by the breeze, a craft that had appeared small and pretty was upon them—hard upon them as the increasingly rough sea flung her violently against the English ship. A fresh, even-stronger swell lifted the Spanish vessel far above, so that her gunwales were higher than the English deck for a moment, and the attacking Spaniards launched pikes and pistol shots down upon the crew of the *Vixen*.

Without further warning, the English privateer was pinned by two Spanish vessels, the urca and the galleass. The hulking galleon swooped down from the west. Her forward guns aimed and fired, missing badly.

There should be a truce, thought Sherwin, now that we have all proven our courage. There was no need to go on with this hazardous conduct. He felt the keen weighty presence of his father just then, not a ghost so much as a memory so true it was both painful and joyous. He experienced his father's calming reassurance, but he also felt his father's trepidation, a wordless prayer that the son not join his father in the life to come.

Sherwin needed more time to consider how to take a life, if the need presented itself, just as a pistol ball struck the gunwale before him, splinters flying, the lead projectile humming past his ear.

Or it would have been a hum if he had heard it, and had

not been suddenly even more completely deaf. He pulled the stiff trigger of his own weapon, and he could feel the mechanism as it whirred and clicked. The blast knocked the firearm off its tripod, and smoke was everywhere.

IN ADDITION to the tumult of combat, the ships themselves struggled, hulls grinding together. The privateer's deck slanted one way and then another as the friction from the vessels on either flank gripped and grated against the English ship. At times the vessels parted, only to have the resulting gaps close in an instant.

It might have been soon after the initial combat, or after an hour—Sherwin could not be sure. But at some point in the late morning, the Spaniards made an attack composed not of lead shot and projectiles but of human beings.

There was no warning, aside from the sound of a trumpet on one of the Spanish ships, a pretty, sharp flourish, a resonance at odds with the cannon fire and smoke. The armed, helmeted force on the adjacent vessel was poised to attack.

The crew of Fletcher's ship thrust pikes, halberds, and axes threateningly across the alternating shrinking and expanding space between the vessels. Men with stone bows—crossbows adapted to discharge rocks—fired down on the helmeted Spanish, and it was clear to Sherwin that Captain Fletcher's crew was eager to fight, and skillful.

"Steady, men," called the captain, as Sherwin's sense of hearing continued to return.

The captain stood, sword in hand, on the quarterdeck, and despite his resolute stance Sherwin could see a look of fervent concern in his eyes—for his crew and for his ship. As his men cried out, challenging the enemy, Sherwin sensed a corresponding loyalty on the part of the crew— for the captain and for the ship he had created from a vision.

The gap once again closed—and the assault commenced.

Sherwin had his sword at the ready when a Spaniard in an iron corselet and gleaming, crested headpiece slipped between the two vessels, and suffered his leg to be crushed.

The accident had been so easy to foresee, and so instantly regretted, that it looked like an act the Spaniard had performed on purpose, to win an ill-advised wager. As the ships parted again, the Spaniard tumbled onto the deck of the *Vixen*, looking all the more fierce for having been already injured, limping badly, and yelling.

Sherwin stabbed him in the throat, doing a poor job of it, not getting a good grip on his rapier, and not driving with all his weight behind the thrust. The Spaniard collapsed. Bartholomew was on the Spaniard at once, stabbing in and out several times with a thin dagger and then leaping away as the Spaniard's companions seized him and pulled the guttering, bleeding man to safety.

Fletcher's crew fought with pikes and axes, countering the Spanish trespassers with a brutal fury. The foreigners retreated as Sherwin lost his own footing. He slipped on blood, falling hard, right beside the seemingly lifeless body of First Officer Highbridge.

HE WAS SHOCKED at the force of his own fall, and even more dismayed at the unexpected condition of the first officer.

Sherwin tried to puzzle through the events that had caused Highbridge to be injured. He had no way of estimating the time that had passed between the first cannon shot and this thunder that shook the ship now, timbers splintering, men cursing loudly. Perhaps they had been fighting for hours. Perhaps he himself was injured. An unpleasant flavor filled his mouth—bile and gall, a graveyard poison. The cabin was a refuge somewhere beyond the smoke.

If Bartholomew had any misgivings about having assisted in killing a Spaniard, he showed none, although in Sherwin's eyes he looked less like a boy than a small old man, smoke-seared and drained.

Lead bounced from the deck, slingshots loosed from the Spanish mast tops, as perilous as any bullet. A splinter sang off Sherwin's corselet, a sound like a flawed church bell.

He felt the blow in his body, in his lungs and in his belly. He knew that without armor he would have been cut in two, and that he was every instant close to losing his life.

33

THE INTERIOR of the cabin was thick with oily dust from the pitch and fiber that had been knocked from the timbers by the reverberating percussion of their own artillery.

Sherwin and Bartholomew staggered into the cabin, carrying the first officer, smoke rising from their sleeves and boots where bits of gunpowder and gun wadding had caught on the clothing. Highbridge was as inert as any human Katharine had ever seen, and her first impression was that he was no longer living.

There was no sign of a wound, but Highbridge was turning a sickened azure hue, his lips sea-gray. Katharine knelt to put her hand on him, feeling for a pulse. A round bruise was appearing on his forehead, like a moon burning through cloud. A pistol shot had struck Highbridge, she guessed, but the bullet had not broken the skin.

She had a memory of Orwell, the ostler's son, who climbed on the roof of the Crossed Keys inn near Fairleigh one midsummer night. He fell off the roof and turned blue, just as blue as Highbridge was this instant. His father had hurried from the barn, knelt, and called his son's name, the youth insensible, lost. But then the ostler had known exactly what to do.

Just as Katharine did now.

She seized Highbridge by the shoulders, and shook him hard and repeatedly, with all her strength—until at last he coughed.

Highbridge took a ragged breath. He opened his eyes and took a long moment to make an inventory of what he beheld. His eyes were bloodshot, and one of his pupils was an outsized ragged oval, and the other a pinprick of black.

He reached up to take Katharine's hand, and his grip was powerless. What he said next made no immediate sense to Katharine, in large part because she could not hear beyond the numbing reports of ordnance that made the *Vixen* lurch.

Highbridge was saying a single word, and it rhymed with *witch. Bitch, itch, flitch.* Sherwin could not understand. Highbridge had suffered a head wound—perhaps his faculties were scattered. To see the formerly upright officer so stricken disheartened Sherwin, and he wished for some power to restore the man to health.

Bartholomew was the first to comprehend.

"He says give the Spanish pitch, sir," said Bartholomew. "Flaming pitch, to start them burning."

SAILORS CARRIED the smoking buckets aloft, and heaved them across the seething water.

A few flaming pails of burning pitch plunged into the abyss of water between the vessels, on either side of the *Vixen*. These errant, fuming buckets sent up spouts of steam and drowned like living entities.

But several flaming projectiles were heaved—by brawn and good judgment—far enough and well enough to annoy their attackers. One bucket was hurled back, and the scattered contents caused alarm, until Sir Gregory and Sherwin joined in stamping out the flames.

The sergeant opened the wooden box of iron bomboes, and he and two able-bodied men were soon setting the fuses alight and heaving the sputtering objects, with their spiraling plumes of smoke, high over the enemy vessels. Sherwin joined them, aware that this was evidence of a suicidal desperation on his part.

He did not feel despair, however, and he certainly did not want to die. His reasoning was that his life was quite possibly already forfeit, his future entirely finished, and that he was as good as food for crabs and eels already. Therefore, he might as well throw himself even further into the fight.

The explosions were earsplitting, and soon the urca and the galleass were both aflame, and the urca was so crippled and so engulfed in fire that the galleon had to break off her attack, in an attempt to avoid entanglement with her fiery sister vessel.

IT WAS MIDAFTERNOON before the character of the day altered from one discordant, violent action after another.

The silence was unsettling—eerie, more stupor than peace.

The bulk of the Armada had swept north and east of Fletcher's ship. The *Vixen* had turned to worry the flank of the enemy force, but remained for the moment out of range of its gunners. The lookout called that Captain Hawkins could be seen, coming up from the west. With the promise of English warships to arrive from the direction of Southampton to the east, there was every sign of a great battle to come.

All this made the present silence more uncanny.

Sherwin was enjoying a pipe of tobacco leaf brought to him by Bartholomew, the fumes snatched away by the wind. He felt that he had never been anywhere but on this ship, and any sense he had of a past, or a future, was little more than a fugitive fantasy. The guns were silent, and the loudest sound now was the breathy thunder of the sails.

"Does tobacco sweeten your humors?" asked Katharine.

"Dr. Reynard," said Sherwin, "swears that it counteracts the effect of gun smoke."

He offered Katharine the mouthpiece.

"No, thank you," she said. "I'll not turn my body into a flue, Sherwin, even if it pleases Dr. Reynard."

Feeling pleasantly rebuffed, Sherwin gave the tobacco pipe back to Bartholomew. Katharine's voice was so unlike any of the sounds that had rent the air that day that he put his arms around her, not solely to embrace her but to keep her just exactly where she was as long as possible.

His iron corselet by then had been removed, although he kept the sword at his hip. He knew his hair was matted and his doublet was wet through with sweat. He had killed a man that day, and he did not relish the truth of that, feeling his own pulse hammer *you, you, you.*

You are living, at the cost of another man's life.

"You're hurt," said Katharine.

"No," he protested, "I am well and happy." He had to laugh—his own voice was a wheezing, unfamiliar sound.

But she reached to his cheek and pulled out a splinter, and found another on the bridge of his nose. He was bleeding from a dozen small cuts, and he had not felt the pain. His right arm ached, too, he realized. The bomboes had indeed been heavy, and he had burned his hand on a fuse.

"My father's hopes," she said, "such as they ever were, are either in the hands of the Spanish or reduced to ash." She spoke sadly, but with a quality of wonder that her prospects could alter so completely in such a short time.

Sherwin believed in that instant that what they were experiencing was an eerie afterlife—something in their souls had been extinguished, leaving their hearts beating.

"Will Mr. Highbridge," asked Sherwin, "soon be joining us on deck?" He made the question sound easy, as though he was certain of an optimistic answer.

The truth was, he feared for the first officer's life.

"He is resting senseless," said Katharine, surprised at the question, "like an effigy of marble."

"Dr. Reynard," said Sherwin, "will surely smoke and drink our good Mr. Highbridge back to health."

"Ah, Sherwin," she said, "I fear not."

Sherwin experienced one more distinct vision of battle that day, and it interrupted a growing illusion of peace. This new violence woke him to the fact that the battle had only begun.

34

THE SUN WAS SETTING, the end of day marred by scudding clouds and the promise of a storm.

Men were making an informal register of shipmates who were still alive, along with a written list kept by Lockwood and his mates. Even Tryce, drunk on wine spirits, made his way to the deck, propped on crutches, to prove that he was alive.

"What a pig cannot kill, no Spaniard will," was Tryce's oft-repeated declaration.

No crew member had been lost. Beer was drunk and savored, and the best wine, and the smoke that filled the air from the galley had a new flavor, mutton and fish the cook had caught the night before, when the day's events were in the future—sole and John Dory, spiced with rare peppercorns from a prize the *Vixen* had taken not a month past.

During this continuing interval of growing security came a reminder of the enemy's power, and his spite.

THE *VIXEN* had continued to drift wide of the main body of the Armada—the wind was behind the Spanish, and the bulk of the ships were bent by force of the weather toward the east. Warning shots from Spanish ordnance stitched the water, but the captain showed no sign of departing from the Armada entirely. The *Vixen* continued her wasp-like presence, stubbornly hovering, but not too close to her powerful enemy.

Burns and blisters were the most common complaints. The surgeon painted gunpowder burns with a balm of sweet lard and carrot pulp, as the doctor explained, mixed with a little suet of cat flesh. Sherwin had received a first application of the ointment after his initial powder burns, and he was already healing.

The captain came aft to survey the minor damage to the ship.

The mainsail was being shaken out, and catching the first full swell of wind, when a cannon shot struck the canvas. The ball had traveled a great distance, but its momentum caused the sail to collapse inward. Sailors had to cling to keep from falling.

The cannonball fell, and hit the deck not a stride ahead of Fletcher.

The ten-pound shot did little damage to the deck, and it rolled slowly, following the camber of the planks, all the way to the scuppers.

"Are you all right, there, Captain, sir?" called Lockwood.

A powder devil, one of the gunner's boys, appeared from nowhere to gather in the lead ball. He was black with gun soot, and seared like a boy who had been pan-fried, but his smile was bright.

"Good lad," said the captain.

Sherwin was deeply relieved to see the captain unhurt.

THE *VIXEN* parted wreckage floating on the sea, all that was left of the *Rosebriar*. A surprising amount of lumber floated on the swells, flesh-colored spans of rough-milled pine. The crew used hooks to gather what they could of this salvage, as well as the bits of sailors' kits and ship's supplies that bobbed on the surface.

Katharine watched over the side of the ship—she and her father had, after all, invested nearly all they possessed in this vessel, and it was appalling to see what a worthy cargo ship of nearly six hundred tons could be reduced to.

The captain examined some of these finds, and called Sherwin and Katharine over to see what had been recovered.

The items made a mournful little cache, so evidently the homely items that individuals had carried for comfort: a velvet shoe, a knit stocking, and a nightcap, along with an assortment of combs of horn and others of bone, wooden buttons and a sodden handkerchief with pretty red stitchery, a gillyflower pattern along the edge.

The entire assembly smelled of pine pitch or turpentine, a valuable cargo but not like the fragrant perfume of cinnamon, and not originating in the balmy tropics, either. Such cargo came from Newfoundland, or some other northern place.

Katharine felt the first stirrings of promise. She did not want to give in to this hopeful feeling, fearful that she might be disappointed.

A plank was carved with the words *Lord is mijn herder.*

It was the sort of sacred phrase a ship's officer or a captain might keep in his quarters. *The Lord is my shepherd,* in Dutch.

"I do believe," said the captain, "that the captured ship was not the *Rosebriar* after all."

35

AFTER HER INITIAL ELATION at this change of
fortune, Katharine realized that she had good reason
to be angry.

Katharine had found the sea battle, which she had
endured from the confines of the captain's quarters, to
have been a period of singular hellishness. For a time she
had sat with a battle pike across her lap, hoping that the
vessel might fall to hand-to-hand combat. That, she had
thought with resentful irony, might at least mean less cannon fire and less likelihood that the *Vixen* would explode
and sink.

Katharine was no innocent about the ways of man and
nature. She had been raised around farmers, and every
farmer is a matter-of-fact killer. When a farmer is not
slaughtering pigs he is castrating them, and when he is
not smoking flesh he is stripping it from bones. Katharine was not weak-willed, and she did not consider herself naïve, but she did feel that battle extended human

violence and recklessness beyond anything the Lord required.

She had told herself that the battle would end, eventually, as God willed, and so here it was—a merciful end.

But the captain showed no intention of departing these bloody seas. His behavior, she thought, bordered on maniacal stubbornness, or perhaps years of gunfire had inured him to the point at which he was dangerous to himself and his crew. If the captain knew the *Rosebriar* was still at sea, why did he not break off the fighting and go seek her? Honor had been established, surely, and there was no need to keep fighting.

"We should try to reach the *Rosebriar*," she said when she joined the captain on the quarterdeck, "and keep her from tangling with the Spaniards."

Despite her relative youth, her counsel was not inappropriate. Her family had a pact with Captain Fletcher, and it was understood that the sponsor of a venture should consult with the ship's captain, as the need arose. But despite her clear, declarative manner, she felt uneasy speaking to Captain Fletcher. She did not trust him any better now than she ever had, and as a woman on a warship she felt the weakness of her position.

"These Spanish great-ships have silken pillows stuffed with rosemary and sweet olive oil," the captain replied. "A Spanish officer has a purse fat with gold reals."

Recognizing her helplessness did not discourage her so much as allow her to experience a sudden mental clarity. Her father had misjudged this man.

The captain was even more unreliable than she had feared. None of these mariners possessed the solid, amiable good sense of a landsman, like Eleanor's husband with his windmill and his practical desire to avoid all hazard. She felt the first glimmer of an uncharacteristic despair.

"Captain," she said, "you are not thinking of sniffing out prizes, surely."

"All are fish," he said, echoing an old adage, "that come to the net."

AS THE EVENING stalled and became one of those vaults of darkness that are not made up of hours but go on endlessly, Katharine became temporarily resigned to what was happening. Besides, it was evident that Highbridge, despite his moments of renewed consciousness, was sinking.

An English ship was expected to hold prayers morning and evening, when conditions permitted. That evening's service was brief, a thanksgiving for their at least temporary reprieve from death. *We gat not this by our own sword, neither was it our own arm that saved us, but thy right hand.*

"For the love of Lord Jesus," prayed the captain in conclusion, "spare our shipmate Peter Highbridge."

FOR TWO DAYS the *Vixen* traded volleys with the southern flank of the Armada.

The English gunners were accurate, within the limitations of their ordnance, but the shot either bounced off

the strakes of the looming Spanish vessels or sank deep
into the enemy superstructures, leaving ruinous-looking
but apparently harmless holes.

Hawkins's fleet of warships joined the battle, and the
Spaniards encountered the bulk of the English fighting
force from the east. A great Spanish galleon burned in the
distance, and Sherwin could see the smaller English vessels darting among the Spaniards.

Fletcher kept his ship near the fighting, but often at a
distance from the greatest tumult. The weather continued
severe, and by the fourth day many English ships had the
weather gauge, sailing upwind from the Spanish and able
to maneuver more freely than their foe. A force with such
an advantage was understood to have the upper hand.

"We're running low, Captain, sir," said Master Gunner
Aiken, approaching the quarterdeck. He spoke with an
economy of words, as though speech were precious
ammunition, too. "We're dwindling on shot, and nearly
out of powder."

Spanish musket balls that fell to the deck were loaded
into sakers and fired back at the enemy.

THAT NIGHT Highbridge could not be awakened to sip
from a posset cup, spiced wine the surgeon had taken special pains to prepare. He lay in the captain's own bunk,
and at first he would respond vaguely, like a man troubled
by a dream, to voices.

"Highbridge," the captain would call, as though speaking to someone at the bottom of a deep well. "High-bridge, old friend, you will stir now, cease this petty malingering, and come out on deck."

Then, as the night wore on, the captain became more urgent. "Damn it, man, we need you. The Spanish are pushed by storm into Lord Howard's fleet. Come on deck, Highbridge, and see the Armada falter."

The surgeon slipped in and out of the cabin. "It is not the shot wound that is the problem," said Dr. Reynard. "I fear that when Officer Highbridge fell, he hit the deck hard, and his head suffered some distemper."

"Have you seen this sort of injury before?" Katharine asked.

"My lady," he responded, "I must say, before God, that more men die of falling on a ship than from minion balls or dudgeons."

She surmised that Reynard was a man of high hope and knowledge, but little power over fate. His surgeon's apron was spotted and dyed, evidently with the gore of his patients of years gone by.

She asked, "Is there no cure?"

"My lady, a hole can be drilled in the skull," said Dr. Reynard, "and the unhealthy humors released, but with the sea so heavy, and the guns firing, there is no steady platform for such a delicate operation."

"SING TO HIM, if you will, Lady Katharine," advised the captain during one of his short visits, "because I have

heard that song can seek the soul and hang on to it."
Katharine sensed that Fletcher would do anything to keep
his friend alive.

But the captain's duties were too demanding to permit
him to remain beside his stricken officer, and besides, the
sight of such closeness to death made the mariner pace
helplessly, turning and turning in the confined cabin, until
there was no relief but to return to the increasing tempest
of wind and rain.

Katharine knew many songs. Almost every act of household labor had a song. Many were carefree, like the one
about the windmill, "Spin my love faithful," and some
expressed superstitions, intended to keep milk from turning sour or to keep a lover faithful.

There were songs for the mortally stricken, too, and so
Katharine sang of the apple that dreamed of the orchard,
and the orchard that dreamed of the kingdom, and the
kingdom that dreamed of Heaven.

Sherwin joined her frequently, when he was able, but
the ship was bounded by turmoil, and resounded with the
calls of the boatswain for men to trim the sails and of the
quartermaster requiring sailors belowdecks. Sherwin was
always needed elsewhere, and it seemed to Katharine that
his visits were all too brief.

HIGHBRIDGE'S respiration began to slacken, until when
Katharine put an ear to his lips she detected only a ghost
of life.

Fletcher sat with his old friend near dawn. For all the trouble he had seen those violent days, and all the lack of sleep, or any other comfort, the captain looked more than anything determined, as though the grime of black powder smoke and the weight of his burdens were met by a corresponding confidence.

"Highbridge, my old shipmate," he said, "you will want to see the Spanish on the run."

Although this assertion was belied, just as he uttered it, by the sound of a shot, skipping across the water. Splashing, splashing closer, and then missing the vessel, leaving Katharine to wonder what harm would fall next.

36

A S MORNING ARRIVED, the ship plunging through heavy swells, Highbridge did not die so much as cease to breathe, and a stillness overcame him. His gaunt, thoughtful appearance altered, and he became empty of life.

HIGHBRIDGE was buried at sea, accompanied by the service prescribed by the Book of Common Prayer, *We therefore commit his body to the deep.*

The crew had congregated, showing deference and sorrowful attention. They had suffered many injuries—hair was singed off by powder burns, splinters had dashed flesh, and some men had to struggle to stand upright. Many eyes were wet.

Afterward, Fletcher called Sherwin to the quarterdeck. "An epitaph is what Highbridge deserves, something in Latin." The captain could barely speak, shaken by emotion.

"I cannot write in Latin, Captain," said Sherwin.

"Of course you can," insisted Fletcher, red-eyed with anger and sorrow. "What lawyer's son is not taught to tell his *veni* from his *vidi*? Highbridge was the finest sailing man I have ever known, and a forthright friend."

"Sir, I can read the language," persisted Sherwin, "but have never tried my hand at writing the Roman tongue."

"Highbridge will have a stone of carved Latin, and you will make up the words," insisted Fletcher, speaking now with determination. "I shall give the marble to a country church in Oddington or Appleton, some out-of-the-way village, the sort I told Highbridge he would retire to."

"As you wish, sir," said Sherwin, sounding resolute, but doubtful of his own talents.

"He would have hated such quiet towns," said Fletcher, "all muddy lanes and chimneys. He was blessed with a seaman's death, and that's a gift indeed." He spoke like a man trying to convince himself.

"But you do not, I hope, plan to give us all such a splendid reward," Sherwin dared to remark, prompted by some inner apprehension.

"Are you afraid I'll sail you to a watery grave?" asked Fletcher with an unpleasant laugh. "Well, we shall see if you will be so lucky."

"Captain Fletcher," spoke up Katharine, "I have an epitaph in Latin, and I recommend it to you."

"A female prodigy," said Fletcher, an unpleasant quality in his voice. "My lady Katharine, you honor us."

"In exchange, you will turn and go back to our point of rendezvous with the *Rosebriar*."

"Will I?" said Fletcher, not in disagreement so much as wonder. "Will I indeed? Or will I prefer to castigate the Spaniards?"

"*Suaviter in modo, fortiter in re.* It is one of my father's favorite expressions."

"Pleasing," said the captain, "and fitting, too. Don't you think. Sherwin?"

"Indeed, sir, a perfect epitaph," agreed Sherwin, not liking the way the captain's eyes cut one way and then another, in barely suppressed fury.

Mild in manner, mighty in deed.

FLETCHER did not sail west to seek the *Rosebriar.*

For the next three days Captain Fletcher took greater risks, seeking to encounter the enemy, even with his supply of powder and shot entirely gone.

At night the *Vixen* sailed close to the struggling Spaniards, and Fletcher looked on as Drake's ship appeared and vanished, more than once, his *Elizabeth Bonaventure* dousing her stern lights so her famous captain could take prizes, sacking Spanish ships undetected except, as it seemed, by the captain and crew of the *Vixen.*

"He's a viper's pup, that Drake," breathed Fletcher.

Sherwin overheard the remark, and he thought that the captain could not suppress a certain reluctant esteem.

WHAT WAS the captain trying to accomplish?

Katharine asked Sherwin, and he said that he wanted to

defend his country, of course, but the words Sherwin spoke were like homilies he had overheard in the past, nothing like his usual warm, spontaneous remarks. Sherwin was too exhausted to perceive what was happening.

Katharine began to wonder if she was the only one who doubted the captain's motives, and if she was insightful or succumbing to the distress of combat herself. She grew increasingly convinced that, in his angry sorrow, Captain Fletcher wanted to see everyone—every mortal on the earth—eradicated.

The ships at nights were shadowy presences hinted at more than seen. The radiance of burning Spanish vessels was cut into by the silhouettes of seacraft attempting to evade danger, or to seek it.

Fletcher gazed out across the darkness. He spoke to no one, and ate and drank but little. His destructive resolve was not evident unless one observed him closely, and took heed of the judgments he made—and the risks he undertook.

37

THE CAPTAIN was resilient and energetic, and he appeared younger than his years, as though the hunger for revenge at the loss of his friend provided a rejuvenating inner fire.

Sir Gregory, on the other hand, leaned on a shattered matchlock, twenty years older in a few days, and Cecil Rawes, the silent Yorkshireman, staggered through the smoke of the swivel guns, exhausted. Even Sherwin had the etched wrinkles and drawn countenance of a man who had slept little.

But if Katharine's long-absent sister, Mary, breathed any advice, it would have been the quietly urged *Trouble, trouble ahead.* The discharge of heavy ordnance had knocked even more of the oakum from many of the planks, and now the ship creaked from every quarter. These groaning timbers sounded like warnings to Katharine, cautions she would be foolish to ignore.

The *Vixen* continued to dog the Spaniards in their increasing disarray, and when an enemy galleon tried to escape and plunge south, struggling through the high seas, Fletcher cut across her course, using the relatively slight bulk of the *Vixen* and the threat of hand-to-hand fighting to drive the would-be fugitive back.

Several times the captain challenged oncoming ships. Each time the advancing vessel shifted her sails and set a course that kept her in the disorganized assembly of her fellow countrymen. And each time this happened, Katharine was convinced that the captain swore under his breath and stamped his booted feet, sorry that the ships had not come together in a grand and mutually destructive collision.

Her suspicions were finally confirmed when the *Vixen* encountered a huge vessel, one of seven or eight hundred tons, and decorated with pennons and flags, the insignia of the aristocrats and knights who manned her.

This grand galleon broke from the Armada and parted the seas directly toward the smaller *Vixen*. And the captain gave a quiet signal: *Stay*.

Stay as we are, directly in her path.

NEITHER SHIP altered course.

Foreign sailors were visible, scarlet sleeves and highly polished armor, with pistols on tripods, the firearms being aimed, steadied, and, as they came into range, fired. The ship stubbornly drew closer, and the *Vixen* did nothing to alter her position, remaining squarely before the looming Spaniard.

The galleon's shadow arrived first, and the smell of her,

not unpleasant so much as novel—a whiff of freshly planed, perfumed wood amid the odor of gunpowder, and pleasing cooking spices, unlike the pitch and sulfur funk of most English ships.

The larger craft slammed the *Vixen* and rocked the smaller vessel, but the impact took place when a swell had lifted both ships, so that the Spanish galleon was approaching up a long slope of water and the English vessel was sliding down the other side.

Even so, the shock was great, and gun carriages shrilled belowdecks, men falling despite their ample preparation. The captain kept a grip on the rails of the quarterdeck, but Sherwin staggered, and searched for something to hang on to as the deck continued to slant. Only the gunwale kept Sherwin from sliding overboard, as Katharine, clinging to the rails near the captain, called out.

The Spanish vessel mounted the side of the *Vixen*, the keel groaning across the gunwales, and with an inexorable logic the upper deck of the *Vixen* began to break down, splinters spinning, the wooden structures giving a shrill, nearly living screech.

The *Vixen* was forced into the sea, her deck awash with water. As Katharine held on to the quarterdeck rail and the captain drew his sword, the English ship went all but under the larger ship with a groan, shuddering and creaking, ratlines trembling. The Spaniards themselves, far from attacking, were more intent on hanging on themselves, cursing the English in their foreign tongue.

Perhaps it was the sight of Katharine, mantled but clearly visible, clinging to the quarterdeck rail, that added to the Spanish hesitation to board and begin hand-to-hand battle. Perhaps the weariness that stunned the English had also altered the will of these would-be invaders. But as the *Vixen* at last spun sideways, the buoyancy of the smaller vessel asserting itself, the Spaniards gazed at their English counterparts with expressions that mirrored Katharine's horror.

A Spanish helmet flashed, a plume flourished in the wind, and a figure on the foreign quarterdeck lifted his hand in a salute, both admiring and dismissive, relieved to be rid of the privateer.

"Fletcher," called a Spanish voice, in surprise, but with the kind of pleasure people feel when they see someone they have beheld only in woodcuts.

At the sound of his own name the captain snapped his sword back into its sheath with an air of satisfaction.

Fletch-air.

The same voice added, in labored, heavily accented English, as though the unfamiliar phrase was quaintly courteous and amounted to a kind of salute: "Captain Fletcher, burn in hell."

Fletcher could not suppress a smile.

KATHARINE COULD NOT contain her fury now.

"My father commissioned this vessel," she told Fletcher. "You are under contract with my family."

"What use is such an agreement here?" asked the captain.

The ship wallowed, masts swaying and creaking, the vessel recovering from the impact, but slowly, a living, ill-treated creature.

"Captain, I formally request," said Katharine, "that you do everything in your power to intercept the *Rosebriar*."

Captain Fletcher straightened his sleeves and brushed the sea foam from the heavy wool. He reached out and brushed a fleck of brine from Katharine's mantle with his gloved hand.

"My duties are legion," he said, iron in his voice, "and I shall neglect none of them."

"Your ship has fought well, and with honor. The Spanish are very nearly ruined. Will you fight until we are all destroyed?"

He gave her a severe smile but said nothing further.

She had a swift insight into what would motivate the man. "How much more of my family money do you want?" she persisted, so filled with feeling that she could not keep her voice from trembling. "If one-third of the *Rosebriar*'s payload will not convince you to live up to your contract, will forty percent? Or as much as half?"

"If your ship reaches the Cornish coast at all, my dear," said Fletcher, "I can seize her and keep everything."

"My father and I need at least half of the proceeds to make good our debts," said Katharine. "But I can offer you my own person as hostage against future payments, if you promise to treat me honorably."

He swept her with a glance that was animated by sexual awareness. His answer was tempered by a knowledge of the responsibilities and challenges involved in maintaining a baronet's daughter both inviolate and secure. "Fortunately for both of us, Lady Katharine, I am not a dragon."

"Are you not?" she heard herself say, in a voice charged with feeling. "Will my prayers be of thanksgiving that God put my life in your care, or entreaties for deliverance from your grasp?"

The crew was listening, as sailors will, pausing in their hurried efforts to steady the ship. Sherwin approached the quarterdeck, looking shaken by the collision, but flushed with relieved vitality. He stopped in his tracks when he caught the full meaning of Katharine's question.

"Two-thirds," said Fletcher in a low voice only she could hear. "Promise me two-thirds, Lady Katharine, and I'll sail west to seek the *Rosebriar.*"

That was too much, she knew.

The price was too high, and yet she had no choice. Besides, the remaining one-third would still do much to restore the Fairleigh larder, and it would pay for the return of house servants, with enough, perhaps, left over for a thriving flock of geese.

Furthermore, Katharine had grown aware of the captain's complexities. He had read the burial service like a man who believed in God, and he looked upon her now as a man with tender feelings, as well as greed.

"Why not take it all?" she said.

I COULD, thought Fletcher.

But even as he was about to utter this threat, the captain felt an unseen companion nearby, breathing *Honor, honor.*

Ah, Highbridge, Fletcher nearly said aloud.

You are reminding me that I am not such a sinner.

Fletcher gave Katharine a smile and a bow, dismissing her courteously. She left his side. One of the reasons he wanted her out of his sight was that she reminded him too well of the young woman in the Fairleigh courtyard. He could love Katharine, embrace her and keep her, and this awareness made him feel protective.

The first threat she would have to be guarded against was his own. He saw her high regard for Sherwin and felt the ancient commander's ruse commend itself: how to put the aspiring historian and poet increasingly in the way of danger.

He motioned to Sherwin now, inviting him on the quarterdeck, and the young man had overheard enough to feel anxious.

"You would not strike a cruel agreement with Lady Katharine, would you, Captain?" asked Sherwin with that quality of assertiveness and optimism that the captain so appreciated. "After all, you wouldn't want the story of your life to be entitled *Avarice.*"

The captain offered a dissembling laugh.

"Give me your word, Captain," said Sherwin, "that you will not harm Lady Katharine or her father."

This time Fletcher's laugh was stony, and he motioned Sherwin away with a curt gesture.

But now the captain sensed that somewhere a second Fletcher—a twin with a career parallel to his—was striding down a country lane, or opening a volume of creamy white vellum, or perhaps memorizing the lines to a great tragedy. Fletcher should have been an actor. Or a man of the cloth, delivering a sermon each Sunday, the silken matrons gazing with uplifted devotion.

He beckoned Lockwood.

Tom Lockwood was an experienced seaman, born and raised in Dover, and yet the man was like a yellow grasshopper, fore and aft in an instant, and he laughed too much.

Lockwood's eyes were eager, his boatswain's call already in hand. Sometimes, thought Fletcher, you had to forgive the living for having survived.

"Lockwood, or I should say Mr. Lockwood," said Fletcher, "I am appointing you my new first officer."

"You'll not regret it, my lord captain," said Lockwood in a burst of high courtesy after a surprised pause. And then he laughed. The man was lousy with merriment.

It wasn't so hard, thought Fletcher, to love your enemy. The challenge, on the contrary, was to be unstinting in the love of your friends. But he laughed, too. Genuinely, happily. Perhaps Lockwood would prove to be a source of good sense and cheer.

The captain said, "We'll set a course west."

SHERWIN JOINED Katharine at the ship's rail.

"I'll see you happy, and see Fairleigh safe," he said.

Katharine wondered if, in his hopefulness, Sherwin understood Captain Fletcher.

"Your lifelong happiness, Katharine, I swear to you," said Sherwin, "will be my desire."

VIII
THE GRIFFIN FLAG

38

THE GRIFFIN BANNER was taken out of Katharine's trunk and brought with quiet ceremony to the deck by Nittany, the newly appointed boatswain.

"With your permission, my lady," said Nittany, who had the voice of a capable house servant, polite and calming.

Sherwin was pleasantly startled at the length and breadth of the banner, a deep blue with the griffin looking back over his shoulder, as though to welcome a following throng. The shadow of the Fairleigh standard fluttered and straightened over the deck, with a rumble like faraway cannon fire.

"Isn't that enough to do us proud, sir?" said Sergeant Evenage, and Sherwin had to agree.

Sherwin was pleased to help the carpenter's mate repair a span of shattered railing on the quarterdeck. The craftsman was a skillful Scot named Magnus Hall, and he wore a belt from which dangled an array of files, hammers, wooden mauls, and clamps. He sang happily as he worked, verses recounting the trials of lost lovers at last reunited. He and Sherwin used a preparation of glue and an artful placement of fastenings to hold a new railing in place, and three hours later it was impossible to detect any former damage.

The crew worked with the precision of adepts in the week after the collision with the great Spanish ship. The pine timbers they had recovered from the Dutch wreckage were put to use repairing harm along her superstructure, and as the *Vixen* coursed westward again, paint was applied to gashes in the spruce-wood timbers, new canvas was run up to replace battle-torn sails, and soon the vessel was very much the deftly outfitted craft she had been.

The cook was able to kindle a fire in his stove, and to provide the entire ship's crew with roast ham and slabs of broiled cheese, along with the best beer and most refreshing cider Sherwin had ever tasted, all served by the ship's steward and his mates, the men responsible for serving food to officers and crew.

But there was still potential trouble.

AN UNFAMILIAR SHIP had been sighted on the southwestern horizon off the Cornish coast, the first vessel in several days. The vessel could be the *Rosebriar*, but she could also turn out to be any of a dozen other cargo ships.

Katharine hesitated. She did not want to make another painful mistake.

This array of sails grew in definition from a mote on the

horizon to a notch against the blue sky. Now it was clearly a weathered yet robust English vessel, with the girth of a cargo ship, but heading at such a straight-on angle that her character, much less her name, could still not be determined. But this likely newcomer was one reason for the display of this reassuring flag. Katharine wanted Captain Loy—if that was who it proved to be—to see at a glance that the *Vixen* was a friend.

The cargo ship was slow, settled deeply in the water.

"Her delay is a hopeful development, Lady Katharine," said Fletcher. "A heavy ship is a rich one."

But as the privateer waited, attending to the ship's repairs, another ship had begun coming up from the opposite direction, from the bearing of Portsmouth, a grand English vessel with red and white paint along her gunwales and newly refreshed white and black gunports.

She had been in recent fighting, judging by the shot holes in her mainsail, but she had been polished and reappointed immediately afterward, to an extent that won the sergeant's admiring "She's been starched and steamed, not a wrinkle in her stockings."

But the crew was apprehensive, too. There was no doubt about the character of this oncoming warship. She was the *Ark Royal*, Lord Admiral Howard's flagship. And as the crew of the *Vixen* looked on, beginning to hurriedly prepare for the unexpected, this notable vessel was keeping a course directly toward the privateer.

The Lord Admiral might be on a mission to chastise

Fletcher for his raids on English prizes, or he might be bent on arresting the captain for some matter of state. There was no limit to the troubled rumors that simmered among the crew, and Tryce hobbled about on his crutches murmuring that they would be justified in ripping a charge of grapeshot across the admiral's bow.

The crew put on their best clothing, carefully mended calico and Bristol cloth, looking in their motley outfits like boatmen on a pleasure barge, Sherwin thought, more than men who had recently battled an armada.

Sergeant Evenage had applied tallow to his boots and belt and looked polished and brushed to perfection. Cecil Rawes had likewise flowered, and the quiet Yorkshireman had purchased or wagered his way into a wardrobe of seaboots, a felt hat with a Cyprus-satin hatband, and a green velvet doublet. Sir Gregory, however, appeared further drained by his recent experiences, and leaned heavily on a pikestaff, looking longingly toward the hint of land to the north.

Sherwin himself was outfitted in a doublet of rare kid-skin leather, a garment Bartholomew had won playing dice in the forecastle. His sleeves were silk plush, indigo-dyed and full, and he wore his mantle like a cape so his sleeves could be admired. He wore the pistol Highbridge had loaned him thrust through his belt—Captain Fletcher had said that Sherwin should keep the firearm, and Sherwin felt both privileged and moved by this gift.

The captain had adopted something like the late Highbridge's manner of clothing, and resembled, in his dark broadcloth tunic devoid of decoration, a scholar, or a man of God.

MORE THAN A FEW MEN eyed the approaching flagship's forward guns, and the darkly gleaming, tightly shuttered gunports, with apprehension. They calculated, as Sherwin surmised from overheard remarks, how many strides it would take to lay hands on their pikes and swords.

Fletcher's crew was prepared for tribute, but they were also ready for strife.

39

"THIS IS DEVILISHLY AWKWARD," said Fletcher.
"Is it indeed, sir?" asked Sherwin.

He felt that he had taken on the role that Highbridge must have filled, responding politely, sometimes pointedly. But Sherwin realized how empty of knowledge and character he was compared with the veteran officer.

"You know it's disconcerting as well as I do," replied Fletcher. "Just as Lady Katharine and I are about to carry out an act of maritime fraud, his lordship decides to pay a visit with an armed guard."

A boat was lowered from the visiting warship, and set out across the easily rolling sea. Care was taken so the oars did not splash, and the rowers were expert, lifting the oars just out of the water, cutting them under the surface again, quietly and with powerful strokes. A gentleman was being conveyed, plumed and garbed in a rich crimson doublet and a buckle with bright gold fittings. The long plume in his cap, and his colorful attire, made him look like a celebrated fighting cock.

This famous maritime administrator, known by sight to everyone who had ever watched the royal barges along the Thames, was accompanied by his personal guard, armored men with halberds and bright headgear—helmets with a gleam rarely seen at sea.

"Have you met the Lord Admiral before, Captain?" asked Sherwin.

"I've avoided the encounter," said Fletcher. "For a professional scoundrel like myself, Lord Howard is the most dangerous official in England."

THE ADMIRAL climbed onto the webbed rope ladder along the side of the *Vixen*, having no trouble with the ascent. The boatswain's pipe sang out its distinctive signal, announcing the arrival of a visitor.

And there he was, looking exactly like the portrait Sherwin had seen at Saint Paul's, where wreaths had been placed to celebrate Drake's raid on Cádiz. If anything, his lordship looked even more splendid than his painting, red-cheeked and keen-eyed. He looked like a man who always picked out the best seat in a tavern, and got it. He slipped off his glove and advanced toward Fletcher.

Lord Howard gave a courtly bow as he was introduced to Lady Katharine, who had put on a white lace collar, with a parcel-gilt griffin pin on her mantle.

"A lady can be aboard this ship to carry out one duty, if you will permit me," said the admiral with a knowing but warmhearted smile.

"And what, my lord," said Katharine, prettily but in a guarded manner, "can that one duty be?"

"Protecting, if I may say, her family investment."

He said this with a quiet laugh, like a man who had uttered a witticism, but when he shot a glance toward the very slowly, distantly approaching cargo ship, Sherwin felt that the *Vixen*'s game was up.

SHERWIN WAS INVITED into the cabin along with the two notables.

No one else was present, aside from Bartholomew, who wore a brushed leather doublet embossed with scarlet stars, a remnant, Sherwin thought, of his days serving as a mountebank's assistant. Bartholomew certainly poured wine with a flourish, and excused himself from the room with a showman's grace.

"I knew your father," said the admiral, gazing at Sherwin with a smile. "He once proposed to me that a ship's dog should be paid a penny for every month at sea, to encourage captains to sail with their pet hounds."

"My lord, my father loved animals," said Sherwin, touched at the remembrance.

"Her Majesty declined to subsidize a navy of dogs," said the admiral amiably, "but she remarked to me that the noted lawyer Morris was a man of good heart. I was sorry to hear of his death."

"My lord," said Sherwin, deeply moved, "I thank you."

"Captain Fletcher," said the Lord Admiral, like a man who changed subject brisky and at his own bidding, "I am happy to set eyes on you."

"You honor me, my lord," said Fletcher, "and my ship."

"Sir John Burgh of the *Roebuck*," said the admiral, "told me of the fearsome strife you undertook, facing down the Armada alone, you and your crew. Yours was the first vessel to engage the Spanish force, and for this Her Majesty is everlastingly grateful."

Fletcher had been sipping his wine with an easy air, but Sherwin had observed the pinpricks of color in his cheeks.

The captain relaxed but little, even now. "My lord, we had little alternative but to serve our own fates and Her Majesty's at the same time. I have no high opinion of my own motives."

The Lord Admiral gave a laugh, like a gentleman who admired a sense of humor. "You, sir, are too modest."

"My lord misunderstands me."

"There will be a knighthood for you, Fletcher, no question about it. You have my word on the matter. I could dub you myself today, but Our Gracious Majesty wants to do the deed herself."

Captain Fletcher looked quietly amazed at the tidings.

"As for the debts—that old business agreement you have with Her Majesty," continued the admiral, "I am ordered to tell you that any understanding or covenant you have with the Crown is hereby rescinded."

Fletcher put a hand to his mouth, going ashen. "Surely this does not mean that I am to be arrested."

It would fit the gloriously high-handed temperament of Her Majesty, thought Sherwin, to promise a knighthood to a man about to be put into chains.

"Arrested for what, Fletcher?"

"For my crimes, my lord," said Fletcher, looking dignified but stricken.

"We are all thieves, dear Fletcher," said the admiral with a cordial laugh. "Her Majesty is the Pirate Regnant, her throne the high command of knavery." He caught himself, and put a confiding finger to the side of his nose. "Although this is not the publicly announced rule, if you understand."

Fletcher chuckled politely and, Sherwin thought, with considerable relief.

"No, I bring you nothing but good tidings, Fletcher," said the admiral. "You are free to get as rich as any man alive. But Her Majesty has a special request for you."

Fletcher was momentarily speechless. "Her Majesty," he said, "can command me and every soul in this vessel."

"You surprise me," said the admiral with a trace of liveliness. "I thought you were a solitary fox, hard to find and impossible to direct. I always believed it. You proved me wrong."

"My lord had the correct impression," said Fletcher with a smile. "But my fortunes have been known to alter."

"Her Majesty wants to send you to Mexico and Southern America, to disrupt the Spanish ports there. She seeks to follow up King Philip's disastrous naval blunder with a strike against his American strongholds. She will reward you, Fletcher, with great generosity. Our gracious Queen realizes that she has until now partly underestimated your value."

"My lord," said Fletcher, his keen spirits now completely recovered, "I should have thought that raids like the one you suggest were more in Drake's line."

"Oh, Drake," sighed the admiral despairingly. "The celebrated Drake took prizes during the sea battle, if you can believe it. He doused his stern lamps and raided Spanish ships—Captain Frobisher complained most heatedly, and I can't blame him."

"My lord," said Fletcher, with perfect blandness, "I am shocked."

"Drake's reputation is besmirched, Fletcher. Quite soiled, for the moment. Her Majesty seeks to send you to America to your great profit in his stead, to the enduring harm of Spain."

Sherwin was thrilled, but at the same time aghast at the fear that Fletcher, through an excess of caution or some seaman's dodge, might decline this opportunity for wealth and adventure.

Fletcher gave Sherwin a glance and seemed to understand the younger man's fears and hopes entirely.

"My gentle associate," said the captain, "would not forgive me if I stepped aside from such a challenge."

But the admiral was already changing the subject, turning to satisfy his curiosity. "And, good Sherwin, what role have you played in this great victory?"

"Is it a victory, then, my lord?"

"Yes, entirely. The Spanish have been whipped by wind and our brave mariners, all the way up around the green island of Her Majesty's kingdom, and even now the remaining vessels are wrecked, I am told, on the Irish coastline. The peasants there cut throats and strip the bodies of the useless Spanish army."

"My lord," said Sherwin, in a voice of hushed compassion, "what a sad end."

The admiral gave a laugh, not of joy, but of suddenly weary acknowledgment, and an atmosphere of heartfelt relief hung over his lordship, making him appear almost humble for a moment.

"Sherwin is going to pen my history," offered Captain Fletcher. "So it can be printed, or staged, as Her Majesty's licensers might allow."

The admiral showed every sign of hearty interest, stirring from his brief reverie. "Will it be like your exceptional *The King of Spain Bearded in His Den and His Staunchest Ships Reduced to Kindling*?"

"My lord," said Sherwin, surprised and gratified that Lord Howard knew his work, "I hope much better."

"A history in Latin, or in English?" asked the admiral.

"In Our Gracious Majesty's own tongue, my lord, if it please you."

"Let's hear some of it," said the Lord Admiral.

Sherwin had not been prepared for this, but he took a deep breath and said,

> *"Until I sing, and name each species*
> *in the garden of my affection, I am desert."*

Both men were quiet.

"Noble lines, although incomplete," said the admiral at last.

"That is always his problem, my lord," agreed the captain.

"But I think," said the admiral with a sympathetic smile, "they are not lines quite made for Captain Fletcher. My good Sherwin, I believe you are in love."

40

IF THERE WAS anything more beautiful than the advance of a sailing vessel, Katharine could not imagine what it might be.

There was no doubt—the weathered ship with the bright new mainmast was the *Rosebriar*, and she was close enough that the figures of men could be seen on the sterncastle, shielding their eyes with gloved hands. A distant cap waved.

Was that small, muted little sound the cry of voices? They were unmistakably happy voices, cheered at the sight of the griffin, and perhaps also by the company of the admiral's flagship.

Nothing can be predicted, she knew. No fortune-teller could foresee what gifts the hours of darkness or the next morning might bring—or snatch away. But as Sherwin joined her on the quarterdeck, she felt his shadow pass across her in the afternoon sun. She felt the protectiveness of Sherwin's hand on hers.

If only, she thought, Fletcher was not going to claim two-thirds of the *Rosebriar*'s wealth. Her father would be badly surprised at the arrangement she had been forced to make, and she did not look forward to telling him.

Her moment of daydream with Sherwin was interrupted by the admiral. His lordship stepped upon the quarterdeck, accompanied by Captain Fletcher.

"You wanted to intercept the *Rosebriar*, my lady, as I guess," said the admiral, "so that she might not fall into the hands of creditors."

Katharine was dismayed. "My lord, you misunderstand."

"My spies, my lady," said the admiral with a quiet smile, "keep me informed of the smallest matter."

The admiral's glance took in the assembled crew, lined up along the deck, but Katharine thought that his lordship gave Cecil Rawes an especially appreciative nod, and that the big Yorkshireman could not suppress a smile in return.

Cecil Rawes had been an individual rarely in her thoughts, a hulking squire who had kept to the shadows. She was shocked at how little she had perceived about him, and about so many things in her life. Katharine felt the already reduced promise of this day slip away even further. "My lord, my father is a principled man."

The admiral leaned close and said confidingly, "And Pevensey is a brute, I understand."

"My Lord Admiral," she said, "perhaps, after all, appreciates my position."

"And how much," asked the admiral, "is Fletcher's share in the *Rosebriar*'s proceeds, if I may ask?"

Fletcher and Sherwin had drawn near, and Katharine nearly blurted out the truth—that the captain would carry off the lion's share.

"The original arrangement was one-third, was it not?" said Sherwin with a purposeful glance at Fletcher. "Surely, Captain, you will prove a man of your word."

The captain gave a grave smile.

Inwardly, however, Captain Fletcher was relieved.

His relief was as deep and complex as any thanksgiving he had ever felt. He was grateful to Providence that in the bitter aftermath of Highbridge's death, the ship and her crew had been spared.

The recent news from the Crown was further cause for joy.

The promised knighthood would brighten his name, and Her Gracious Majesty's willingness to allow Fletcher a larger share of future winnings was welcome, too. But as for any grand scheme to raid Spanish galleons in American waters—Fletcher would wait and see what developed. He did not want to make Drake's mistake of hunting more birds than he could kill.

What added to the captain's relief was the fact that Lord Howard had not asked to inspect the ship's private account books, nor did he ask to examine the contents of Fletcher's strongboxes. Fletcher had poured gold into Her Majesty's treasury, but he had cheated her, too. Little by little, over the years, the captain had kept back more than his legal allotment. He had shared these embezzled riches with his crew, and in fair portions, but Fletcher knew that traitors had been disemboweled, castrated, and beheaded for lesser crimes.

"That *was* the understanding," said the captain at last.

He was all too aware that Sherwin and Katharine could embarrass him in the presence of Lord Howard, and yet there was a further reason Fletcher was pleased to reduce his share.

Like a man hiding a fault from himself, Fletcher was succumbing to warm affection for Sherwin and Katharine. He wished them a long life together, safe from men with fewer scruples than his own. He was relieved to find a way to frustrate his own greed.

"Lady Katharine," he added, "I shall be pleased to share one-third of the *Rosebriar*'s prize, as we agreed at your father's table."

Katharine clasped her hands together in joy.

The Lord Admiral glanced at Captain Fletcher. "You'll bring the *Rosebriar* in to Southampton, under my care." He inquired of Katharine, "The vessel is conveying cinnamon, as I have been told, is it not?"

"And dyestuff," she said, feeling the increasing stirrings of hope. "Brazil wood and logwood."

"The cargo," he said, "will be under Her Majesty's seal."

Katharine was afraid that she might have misunderstood, and she faltered. "Are you, my lord, impounding our shipment?"

Lord Howard looked authentically dismayed. For an

instant he lost the jaunty if overbearing quality that matched the angle of his plumed cap, and he looked like an official exhausted nearly beyond patience.

"What ill-treatment you expect of Her Gracious Majesty," he said.

Katharine put a hand on his arm. "These last days, my lord, have tested all of us."

He gave her a fatigued but appreciative smile. "My lady Katharine, I am arranging to purchase the entire cargo on behalf of the Crown. I promise you that in her pleasure with Captain Fletcher's brave service, the Queen's price will be generous."

Katharine allowed herself to feel happiness again. "You, my lord, are a godsend."

"Perhaps," said Lord Howard. "But Her Majesty will be pleased to have a monopoly on all the cinnamon and dyes in London for the next few months. Think what a profit she will make!"

AS THE *ROSEBRIAR* approached, Sherwin watched the gulls spin and wheel, touching down on their reflections in the shifting, mirrored blue of the sea.

If there was one shadow across his happiness, it was that his father would never know Katharine.

But as the crew of the *Rosebriar* heard the news of England's victory, delivered in clear tones through Captain Fletcher's speaking trumpet, they cheered. This happy sound reached back across the water, *God save our Queen* sounding like quite a different message.

The ring.

Give Katharine the ring.

The signet ring, with the greyhound symbol. If his father had been alive to speak, that would have been his message.

A GREAT PUFF of white appeared along the prow of the *Rosebriar*, the merchant vessel firing one of her forward guns. The sharp report of the brass piece resounded through the light afternoon winds, and Katharine was taken aback.

"It's a salute," Sherwin reassured her with a laugh, "a signal of joyfulness."

As the *Rosebriar* swept forward, leaving her smoke to settle on the water, Sherwin placed a circlet of gold in Katharine's hand.